FORTY STORIES

Paul Beckman
& Zvi A. Sesling

ISBN: 978-1-945917-87-5

Printed in the United States of America

"Making other books jealous since 2004"

Big Table Publishing Company
San Francisco, CA
www.bigtablepublishing.com

Table of Contents

I. Paul Beckman

II. Zvi A. Sesling

Paul Beckman

These stories have been published in the same name or another, and they are made up by me. Many families have some similar stories in their history. Thanks to all the publishers and magazines that have shared these adventures with me. My thanks to my wife Sandra and my son, Joshua Beckman, for being my sounding board and editors.

A Flock of Mortimer Snerds

My family started with the giggles as soon as they sat down. The goofball cousins tried to take the first row but were ushered out and they moved behind us to the third row.

I didn't want those freaks sitting behind me.

The aunts and uncles came in—the aunts all lipsticked and rouged up wearing new hats they thought made up for their old dresses for this special occasion. The aunts were actually smiling, something not seen all that often whereas the uncles always had a goofy look that made them appear to be smiling. I don't know how the hell all six sisters ended up with a flock of Mortimer Snerds. Some might say they were lucky to end up with anyone being the toughsters they were.

Other people walked in solemnly and dressed in new suits and hats both the men and the women, and the kids in white starched shirts and bow ties. One of the women took over and pointed at rows for people to sit in and she didn't have to holler or hit anyone they went where they were pointed. You couldn't find a smile in the lot of them. The looked straight ahead and sat upright and no one fidgeted or gave an Indian rope burn to a cousin not like what was going on in our side of the church.

My family was so happy with this upcoming wedding and theirs was equally unhappy, maybe more so. We acted like we were the one marrying into money not just Bernie who could've cared less about the Potters and their money. The Potters were unhappy about marrying beneath their status and a Jew to boot. My family didn't know squat about Episcopalians except that soon there was going to be a mess of them in the family.

The wedding was scheduled for noon, and it was ten after and people were still straggling in which didn't make my uncles very happy. They ate by the clock and right now the clock was telling them they were hungry. They wanted the ceremony to be over and to be in the Elks Club for the bounty that Mr. Potter was sure to have.

The Rabbi and the Minister came out from behind the curtain and neither looked happy and wouldn't until the ceremony was over, and they were given their envelopes. The organ player played a song, and we looked around for the monkey since none of us ever saw an organ player without one. Mom and Bernie walked up the aisle first and stood in front of the clergy guys and Mom stepped back two steps and waited.

Next a little girl carrying a basket walked up the aisle and tossed out rose petals as she went and when her basket was empty, she stood still, and the organ grinder played "Here Comes the Bride." Teens in tuxedos escorted girls in gowns up the aisle and then Mr. Potter and Missy walked up stopping every other step. She was beautiful. Bernie turned to greet them, shook Mr. Potter's hand, and then took Missy's hand and they stood facing the clergy guys.

Mr. Potter took two steps back and then, since his legs were no longer than Mom's, took a half step forward and they stood side by side not looking at each other. The Rabbi said mumble mumble mumble, and then the Minister said his mumbles and then the Rabbi put a 30-watt light bulb in a napkin and Bernie stomped on it and Mom almost jumped into Mr. Potter's arms as half the room (Bernie's half) yelled Mazel Tov and clapped. Then Bernie kissed Missy and Mr. Potter shook Mom's hand and our side piled out while the other side stayed in their seats until the pointer lady pointed at them to go.

Bernie and Missy held hands as they walked to the Elks Club, and we all followed them. Inside the Rabbi mumbled over the loaf of braided bread and the Minister mumbled over the wine and then the band started playing while waitresses passed around food from large platters and then the hushes broke out as Bernie and Missy danced while everyone stood around the dance floor and watched. After a bit Bernie took Mom's hand and danced with her and Missy danced with Mr. Potter and then Bernie and Missy went back to dancing, and

Mom walked over to Mr. Potter and put her arms out and he danced with her. I tell you that they were way better at this dancing thing than Bernie and Missy.

Someone announced that the bar was open, and people lined up to get their free drinks. The band stopped playing and Mr. Potter made a short speech welcoming Bernie into his family and Mom followed him and said, "Welcome, Missy. We love you." Then Mr. Potter took the mic and said, "The open bar will close in a half hour and dinner will be served."

Another Train Ride

As we approached New Haven Station you walked up towards the front of the car, near my seat, waiting for the train to stop. It moved slowly, in herky-jerky motions. You bent down and looked over my shoulder to see out the window. My wife continued to read, but I turned my head and saw your beautiful young face, you were maybe twenty, twenty-one, tops.

I saw the smoothness of your soft brown hair, the color of a cow's eye, the same color of my Anna's hair many years ago before it became the gray and white streaked wrapped in a bun hair. Your hair, with its incredible shininess, turned up a bit at the ends to frame a face, a face beautiful enough to be framed.

Our heads were less than a foot apart at times, but my Jew Face was invisible to you or might as well have been. I smelled your girl smell, your Wasp smell, and noticed your hair splayed across your forehead like accent marks. You held on to my armrest as you peered down the tracks. The almost invisible hair on your very white arms caused me to turn and look at my Anna's arms.

You stood and then bent, once again, leaning over me, poaching on my space as if it were communal. Your presence implied that by looking out the window you could make the train speed up. And each time you did that I stared at you.

You never noticed me, either sitting or staring, as if someone like me, with a Jew Nose much larger and so different from your own perfect little girl's nose, was not worthy of being noticed. And there was no possibility that your actions could be misinterpreted for anything other that what they were. They acknowledged my invisibility by suffocating me into my seat.

Those sweet and naturally pink lips, upturned at the ends, had never felt the need or desire to snarl or sneer the way my Jew Mouth had been forced to snarl and sneer back so often in my life. Your beautiful hazel eyes, with long lashes, didn't notice me noticing you, no matter how long you stayed bent over or how close you came to my Jew Face.

Saying, "Excuse me," was not tendered to the likes of me. It would be more like me to say it to you as my way of hoping to back you off, to give me my air, but the words remained crammed inside me.

I looked over at Anna again, at her spotted and dark arm and the discoloration above her hand holding the book, and then I looked at your delicate wrist surrounded by several fine gold bracelets.

I knew you filtered out anything you didn't perceive to be good and positive and of your world, which to you was one and the same. Other yous, that is all you wanted to see or associate with. That is what you were raised to see, that and nothing other, no matter how close or how many. The homeless and ethnics might just have well been accouterments to buildings, for they were so invisible to you. Yet my Jew Eyes looking through my rimless glasses, resting on my Jew Nose saw those people first.

Finally, the train pulled to a stop, and I watched as you disappeared into a crowd of your people, not noticing any of my people, of which there were many, swirling around you on the New Haven platform.

Anna patted my hand as if to say, "I was that young and pretty once." With my free hand I patted her back, telling her that I knew.

Scrub-A-Dub-Dub

"Can you believe our good fortune?" Beth said to her husband as they looked in the bassinette. "He's so beautiful."

"Who would have thought it?" Martin said. "I was afraid he was going to come out looking like me."

With tears in their eyes, they hugged. Baby slept.

The next week the families came for the bris. The aunts oohed and aahed while the uncles talked amongst themselves and noshed. Two weeks later they had a party for their friends.

"Can you believe it?" Martin said, "That Beth and I, homely as we are, could have such a beautiful baby?"

"With our looks, what were the odds?" Beth asked. "Here. Look at our baby pictures."

And Beth showed her and Martin's baby pictures and it was true they were no beauties, and just as adults their noses and ears were accentuated and the smiles lopsided.

"Who would have thought that a baby from the two of us could be so beautiful? Martin asked, his arm around Beth's shoulder.

Their friends said all the right things and kitchy-cooed and aahed all over the place, but in fact saw a baby who combined the most prominent features of both parents and who was anything but beautiful.

As they lay in bed, Beth, and Martin each wondered if the other knew.

Badges of Mourning

Sarah safety-pinned on her dress a piece of cloth from her mother's apron, a corner off her father's tallit, and a piece from her brother's baseball uniform. Then, leaving the hotel, she took a cab to the synagogue.

Inside, she walked down the aisle approaching the caskets and spotted the Rabbi. She walked over. She told him she was Sarah and took her coat off. Please rip these ribbons and say the blessing she said pointing at her handiwork. He asked the meaning of each. She told him.

They were outside the doorway of the ante room holding the mourning family, leaving room for well-wishers. The Rabbi reached into his pocket and took out a black ribbon, but Sarah insisted on three black ribbons with safety pins and one by one he pinned a black ribbon and said a prayer after cutting the ribbons up the middle with a scissors. He said the English and Hebrew names of her sons and her husband who lay in the caskets, but he did not touch the safety pinned pieces from her parents and brother who sat in the mourner's room looking at her. They hadn't seen each other in the five years since she'd walked out on her family to be with another.

The Rabbi motioned for her to go into the mourner's room to be with the family before starting the service, but she turned and walked to the caskets and stood dry-eyed and motionless, head bowed, hands on each casket, lips moving until she was gently prodded away so the funeral service could begin.

Argyle Nights

"If you loved me, you would fight with me—you would at least argue with me—you wouldn't just sit and stare," my late wife Ellen would say. "Don't you care enough to argue, to raise your voice? What kind of man doesn't have a strong point of view? Or any point of view? I'll tell you," she would say. "A man with no love in his soul. A man with no soul. That's who. That's who you are."

Before that period of our life Ellen would say to me. "Stop fighting with me all the time. Can't you ever go along? Why does everything have to be a debate with you? If you loved me, really loved me, you would let me have my way occasionally instead of fighting me at every turn."

Neither approach worked with Ellen. I tried to change, I did change, but what good did it do? I was wrong no matter which way I turned and on August fourteenth *everything* began to change. Once the change began to happen it couldn't be undone. I didn't know it then, nor did Ellen. On August fourteenth I began building my fence.

I was sitting in our living room on my lounger being berated by Ellen for whatever, when off in the distance, through the living room window I saw a stack of white pickets piled high in large, neat piles. As her voice droned on, I visualized myself walking across the yard to the pile taking a picket and returning it to the living room. Ellen was continuing her harangue when I came back, and just before I sat down in my lounger, I looked at Ellen, picked up a hammer that happened to be lying on the floor, and hammered in my first picket between us. And suddenly, her voice was not quite as grating.

The next time Ellen got on my case was in the supermarket. I walked away and found the pickets section, selected another, and turned to face Ellen. I hammered it in next to the first picket. I had not planned it this way, but somehow, I knew that once the picket fence was complete, our marriage would be over. Oddly enough, I never thought about the picket fence or visualized it unless Ellen was bothering me. And then on a two-picket day I could see the pickets in the horizon of my peripheral vision taking shape as a fence from my right. The pickets proceeded from right to left like the Kaddish. One day there were a few lonesome pickets and then they became the makings of a fence. I was fencing Ellen out of my life or vice versa.

We had our ups and downs and at one point we went through a very rough period that brought the fence midway. This was followed by a long, quiet, loving time when no pickets were added, but make no mistake about it, I never considered removing any. These good times were just temporary, I knew.

Even though I never thought about the fence at other times, whenever I saw Ellen, the white picket fence was between us in some stage of construction.

For a while I feared that I was turning into my brother. He was keeping a loose-leaf notebook on stupid, irritating, and annoying things that his wife did. Once the notebook was filled, he planned to leave her. "A man should only have to take so much in his life," my brother said, "and I have decided that my allotment is this loose-leaf".

He always carried with him a small pocket sized spiral and each evening he would sit in his lounger with a glass of Old Overholt and transfer his daily notes into the loose-leaf. Often his wife was right in the room with him, knitting or watching tv, and if she happened to say something stupid, irritating, or annoying my brother would shake his head and add it to his list. Sometimes he only wrote a sentence and at other times he wrote pages. He often offered to let me read his looseleaf to gain my sympathy for his plight, but I told him I'd wait for the end and read it as a novel. My brother's wife, she was stupid. She should have let him finish the book and divorce her so she could get on with a more normal life. She would sneak into his desk and add blank pages to the loose-leaf every so often. She should have been ripping them out instead.

My brother was critical and compulsive and very vindictive, and I tried to relate his looseleaf notebook to my White Picket Fence. I concluded that there was no association whatsoever. My brother was off the wall. And I, like his wife, was the victim.

Incredible as it may seem, my brother made no secret of his journal. He told anyone and everyone who would listen, never understanding what a bad light it shed on him. I told no one of my fence.

One day I came home late from work, bursting with good news about business, but Ellen would hear none of it. She was irate and from the top of the stairs threw my clothes over the railing and into the hallway. With each toss a picket went up. And that night I finished my fence.

The next day Ellen was dead.

I moved all my belongings into the den and guest room and did what any good Jew would do for the dead. I stayed home from work and sat Shiva—mourning for a week. I tore my shirt, didn't shave, wore a black arm band, and covered the mirrors with sheets. I took the pillows off the chairs so I would not be comfortable, and I said the Kaddish morning and evening.

The next week, a widower, I went back to work. Nothing else changed in my life except that now when I came home from work, and Ellen talked to me, I didn't have to pay any attention because she was dead. Period. Oh, Ellen carried on for a while, even refused to make my meals and do my laundry, but I held my ground and said nothing. After all, what good does it do to argue with the dead, especially if you couldn't argue with them when they were alive.

Ellen came around. It took about six months, but she finally realized that I was never going to speak to her again and for me she was no longer living. She went back to cooking and cleaning for the two of us. We even went to some family functions together and never spoke. Ellen never liked me that much anyway and was probably just sore that she hadn't thought of it first. Divorce?

Don't ask. Divorce was out of the question.

Of course, the only one in my family that said anything to me at all was my brother. "Are you nuts?" he asked. "You just can't declare someone dead and go on living with them."

"Why not?" I asked.

My brother looked up and asked, "Do you plan to date?"

Ellen and I had been married for eighteen years and we, like many other couples, had fallen into a regular routine. She would lay out my clothes for me every morning while I was in the bathroom, and I would wear whatever she selected. Both of us agreed that her taste was superior to mine in the world of fashion. Early on in our marriage, strictly by coincidence, she had put out argyle socks for me on a day that we had made love. Argyles had become our signal and it was always Ellen who initiated the schedule. I had not given much thought to lovemaking since her death, so finding the argyles set out one morning kind of threw me off kilter. I didn't know how to react or what to expect.

It wasn't just argyles and jump in the sack night. There was a ritual, even for us. A nice meal with a glass of wine and then I would pour two glasses of wine and Ellen would bring them to our respective nightstands while I showered. She would sip half of hers and then while she showered. I would sip half of mine. After we made love, we would lie next to each other, bodies touching, holding hands and sip the rest of our wine and go to sleep.

I didn't know what to expect this argyle night. At first, I thought that Ellen had put out the argyles by mistake, but Ellen doesn't make those kinds of mistakes. I came home from work and could tell by the smells when I entered the house that it was an argyle night. Brisket and potatoes air met me at the door, and for dessert Ellen had made her apple strudel. We drank a couple of extra glasses of wine with dinner, but even that didn't loosen my tongue enough to talk to a dead woman. I lingered longer than usual because of my uncertainty on how to end the evening.

Force of habit had me pouring two glasses of wine afterwards and I didn't know if they were going to her room, my room, one in each or what. Ellen, not surprisingly, took control. She carried the glasses to my room, formerly the guest quarters, and ran my shower. I soaped with anticipation and not wanting to seem too eager I took my time in the shower. When I came out, I saw only my glass of wine on the nightstand.

Ellen was not there. I lay on the bed for quite a while sipping my half glass of wine figuring that she was showering and getting ready. I waited for her return but after a while it became apparent that she wouldn't be coming back. I finished my wine, fell asleep and dreamt of Ellen and the argyles.

In the morning I dressed in the clothes that Ellen had laid out for me. For breakfast she made corned beef hash and poached eggs, my favorites, just as she always had after an Argyle Night. And she never even looked at me as she sipped her coffee, nor said a word.

Bedtime

It's a quarter of seven and time to put Ari to bed or my daughter will be all over my case and blame me if he's late getting up in the morning and cranky from lack of sleep, and he only wants to watch the end of this stupid Hannah Montana program and Zeyde, he says, one of us has to stay and watch it and let me know what happens, and I ask him if he's seen it before and he says at least six times so I tell him then he knows what happens, but he comes back with his seven-year old logic and says that maybe something different is going to happen because we're watching it on a different night and he's watching it with his Zeyde and no, the mean baby sitter who won't read to him if they watch it until the end, and he asks me if I'm going to read the next chapter in his book on the Titanic and I say I will but I might have to start it while he's in the tub taking his bath, and he asks who's going to scrub-a-dub-deb him if I'm reading and I tell him of course he's right so I tell him I have an idea and he gets all excited about an idea he doesn't know yet and I tell him I will give him a speed bath, speed dry, and he will do a speed brush teeth and then we'll speed into the bathroom, and I'll do a speed read of the Titanic chapter, and give him a speed tuck in and speed hug and kiss and yes he can tell me a speed joke and I tell him okay as long as it's not that knock knock banana joke, and he says aww that's his favorite joke and I speed carry him upstairs and I feel the ache in my old knees, and speed undress him and all the while the tub is running, and I stand him in front of the toilet so he can speed pee, and toothpaste his star wars toothbrush, and hand it to him and tell him to speed brush and hurry up and pee because if his mother gets home, and he's not sleeping by seven thirty then she won't let Zayde babysit anymore and bad Bubbeh will be his sitter and he knows what that means and finally he pees and I speed grab him and put his pjs on and speed tuck him in and start to speed read from where the bookmark is and I hear my daughter's car pull into the garage and speed up my reading but thankfully all this speed has worn out my grandson so I know I won't be denied any more from my former wife and I kiss him on his head and head for the door while I hear a sleepy voice say, Zayde, knock knock. . .and I speed my way out of his bedroom after turning on his nightlight and close the door behind me, and I check my watch, and I had two minutes to go so I start down the stairs to face the barrage of mother questions.

Mrs. Brophy's Jews

Come into the house, the old lady said. I won't hurt you. It's my seventy-fifth birthday today.

Happy birthday I said, as I stepped by her into the living room. And, I smiled, I'm not afraid that you'll hurt me.

Well, I could if I wanted to, she said screwing her face up as she spoke. Go on into the kitchen. Go ahead. She made pushing movements with her hands.

There was a path between the stacks of newspapers that I began to follow with her right behind me clicking her teeth as she walked. The papers were almost five feet high—just about the woman's height. Looking over them I saw that they filled the room. I looked around as I walked and saw cobwebs, huge ones, in every corner and I could feel my allergies creeping into my sneeze passages.

Something to drink, she asked after we both entered the kitchen, which was shiny clean with empty countertops save for a small TV but not a newspaper to be seen. She opened the refrigerator and I saw it was neat, barely filled and had everything either wrapped in plastic wrap or in Tupperware. She brought out a carton of milk and a Tupperware container, walked to the cabinet and brought back two glasses and sat down. She poured milk for the two of us and then opened the plastic container and showed me an almost full package of Oreos. She took one, dunked it in her milk and bit from it.

Well? She asked. Are you going to let me eat my birthday cookies alone?

I couldn't do that, I told her and grabbed, dunked and bit into a fresh Oreo. I tried to remember the last time I'd dunked a cookie but couldn't. I took another and soaked it in the milk. I felt like a kid back in my grandmother's kitchen.

Don't get too cozy with those, Mister, she said. They don't grow on trees.

But I still have some milk left and it's your birthday I said.

Yes, but it's not your birthday, she said wagging her finger at me.

Last one I said grabbing a cookie as she was pulling them away from me.

You're a quick one, you are. Tell me again why you're here. It better not be for my land.

As a matter of fact, Mrs. Brophy, I am here about your land. I'd like to buy it.

Go on. Get out of here. Where will I go? Do you land people ever think about that? Of course, not she answered. And to think I wasted my birthday celebration on you.

It wasn't wasted, Mrs. Brophy. I took out a roll of lifesavers, peppermint, and offered her one and she took it.

Don't think that'll soften me up she said softening her tone. You can't sweet-talk me with sweets. She laughed at her own joke and took the roll and put it in her apron pocket. What's your name? Why don't I know your name? Did you tell me already?

Well, I did on the phone but that was a couple of days ago. It's Mirsky. My name is Mirsky.

What's Mirsky? Eyetalian? Jew?

Jew, I said.

You sure you're not a Jew lawyer? Wouldn't have any other kind of lawyer.

You shouldn't have any other kind of land man either I told her in a confidential tone.

I'm busy, Murky. Time for you to go.

We haven't spoken yet, Mrs. Brophy, and it's Mirsky.

Don't correct me, Murky. Have respect for your elders. Once again she laughed at her own wit.

I respect you and that's why I want you to hear me out I told her and then continued before she could get in her next shot. I want to buy your land but you won't have to worry about where you're going because you can stay in this house as long as you want.

Fifty years?

Even sixty I said.

What's the catch?

No catch and I told her how much money I'd give her and that she could stay in the house for the rest of her life for free, I'd even pay the taxes.

Let me think about it she said but you can call Bernstein and tell him.

I take it Bernstein's your Jew lawyer.

Don't be dumb she said Bernstein's my Jew accountant. Slotnick is my Jew lawyer and now I can say that Murky's my Jew land man.

Two months later we three Jews were sitting around Mrs. Brophy's kitchen table signing papers and dunking Oreos. I slid her a roll of lifesavers that rapidly disappeared into her apron pocket. It had become as much a ritual as the Oreos, and I never changed from peppermint for fear of setting her off. She pulled a piece of paper out from her pocket and handed it to Slotnick and told him to call the name written down and twenty minutes later Mr. Pin Stripe Suit walked into the kitchen with his briefcase and sat down.

Meet my Jews, Junior, she said to James Wolcott III, the bank president as she handed him the check. Wolcott didn't introduce himself but nodded and got up saying goodbye only to Mrs. Brophy and walked back out.

Barrel of laughs she said reaching for an Oreo, barrel of laughs and she laughed once again at her own joke.

We Jews got up, said our goodbyes to Mrs. Brophy and left, all going our separate ways. I looked back at Mrs. Brophy's house and she was standing in the doorway. She motioned me over. I was always told you guys stick together she said.

That's only in the movies I told her. What's with the newspapers I finally asked her?

Mr. Brophy, God rest his soul, said to keep them for a rainy day.

Well with all your money now you won't have to worry about that, will you?

I'm kind of used to them now but if you know someone who'll haul them away I'd appreciate it.

No problem I said. It's been a pleasure doing business with you.

I'll let you in on a little secret she said and covered her mouth as she laughed. I'd have sold you my land for less money, a lot less.

That's okay, Mrs. Brophy, I said and winked at her. I'd have paid a lot more for it.

Her smile gone, she reached into her apron pocket and pulled out a roll of peppermint Life Savers and handed it to me. She turned and went back into her house. I popped a Life Saver and drove off.

Bubbe Replacement

My Cousin Reba's mother and dog both died in October of last year. The dog went first (he was seventeen). Her mother, just a few weeks shy of eighty. One death had nothing to do with the other. At the evening Shiva call people sat around talking and eating after saying Kaddish, and the conversation got around to whether Reba was going to replace her dead dog with a new one. Her three children listened without giving their opinions.

Reba surprised everyone by saying that she was more interested in replacing her mother than her dog. "I won't miss the dog, but will miss talking to my mother, and I'm planning to go to the Jewish old age homes in the area and interview for a substitute. The major criteria being a woman with no family, or with family that never visits or calls. I'd prefer someone who gives advice, comments on my weight and clothes, and always says what's on her mind," Reba said. "If she's a complainer that'll be even better," she added. "I want someone as much like Mom as possible."

The assembled thought Reba was kidding and when she left the living room the Rabbi took the opportunity to tell the friends and family that she was in a state of what's called, *Shiva Shock*. "I've seen this before," he said. "Believe me. It's not that uncommon," he said stroking his beard attempting to appear worldly and wise. He looked neither.

That made her kids feel better until the following month when they all got together at Reba's house for a Sunday dinner and were introduced to Ida, who was a resident of the New Haven Jewish Home for the Aged. During dinner she complained to Reba that the soup was too salty and the brisket just a little bit tough and asked her to please turn up the heat.

Reba, with a satisfied look on her face, told her kids that Ida was the latest in a series from the "homes" that she'd had over as a "tryout."

After dinner Reba's two sons went off to a party and her daughter drove Ida home. On the ride Ida said, "You should get your mother a dog, nothing too big, but a nice dog for companionship, maybe a poodle. I used to have a poodle so that would be nice, and she could bring her when she comes to visit me. You have a pretty face," she said to Reba's daughter, "But a little lipstick wouldn't hurt. And you could lose a few ponds and consider a nose job."

A Part of The Landscape

The letter came and Diana tossed it on her counter with the flyers and magazines but took the huge envelope that had to be an invitation to a wedding—probably, she hoped, her daughter's.

With a joyous heart she stuffed it in her purse to open and enjoy with her morning coffee after her gym workout. Diana and her daughter, Becca, had been estranged for several years and all her attempts to make things right had gone unanswered.

She whipped through her workout and added ten minutes of cardio to savor the invitation opening. She needn't have bothered. While sitting with her coffee in the corner of her local coffee shop, she pulled the invitation from her purse. It was an invitation to Becca's wedding alright, but in every conceivable place was written in **NOT**. *You are* **Not** *invited to the wedding of Becca and* . . . The return card was filled out for her. *I will* **Not** *be attending*. . . The meal choice was filled with a dash as was the brunch the next day. Written at the bottom of the non-invitation invitation was a note; *Please read the letter that came in the same days mail for an explanation. B*

The letter stayed unopened on Diana's counter for so many days that she no longer saw it—like a pair of socks on the stairs waiting to be carried up to the laundry they just become a part of the landscape after a while.

The following month, on the day of the wedding, Diana opened a bottle of gin, and poured herself a glass; her first in over three years of sobriety and sat down to read the letter.

Mom, I sent you that invitation so you can feel some of the hurt that you have unleashed on me over the years. Your years of drinking and the embarrassment and humiliation it's caused me personally and professionally have made me your bitter angry child. But now I've gotten over that, and I want you to know how proud of you I am for sticking with your clean life and I want you at my wedding to walk down the aisle with me. It will mean so much to the both of us—I just know it. I love you. Your daughter, Becca.

Diana was crying by the time she finished the letter and looked over at the clock. It was blurry and she couldn't make out the time but she knew that her daughter needed her so she got up and staggered to her bedroom, leaving the almost empty gin bottle on the floor, to find something to wear that would pass as a mother-of-the-bride dress and hurry to the Synagogue where the wedding was taking place. Unfortunately, she made it in time driving fast and erratically without the good fortune of being pulled over and arrested as she had so often in her past.

Gammerman's Choice

Gammerman knew that he shouldn't send the email, he even paused and said to himself, "Gammerman, don't send that email." And then he hit the send key. That in a nutshell is the story of Gammerman's life, he always knew what his choices were, and when push came to shove, he took the one most harmful to himself.

And, like many others in his life, this choice couldn't be undone even if he wanted to. There was no way to recall the email, not that he considered doing so for even a nanosecond.

"Wait a day, Julius," his mother always said, "and then mail the letter, but wait a day first." His wife would tell him not to make the call in anger, but to wait a day or two. He never understood the rationale behind that thinking because he knew he would be just as upset the following day, maybe even more so since he let things fester, and then he'd only want to toss the letter and write a stronger one. Gammerman never regretted anything. Period.

Gammerman was a strange one, alright. The more his actions came back and bit him in the ass, the more he blamed other people for putting him in that position, and like a dog with a bone he wouldn't let go of his anger or hostility no matter what or how long.

Gammerman left a trail of his own bones that could be carbon dated back fifty years, but yet, those that knew him were still caught off guard when they received the email telling of his anger at all of them for not acknowledging his sixtieth birthday—a milestone birthday at that, and to thank them he wanted to share a little tidbit, some gossip or perhaps a secret about each and every one of them that would be informative to their spouses or friends in the group and that included his wife. He wanted them to know how hurt he was and for them to share in his hurt.

It was effective. So much so that they canceled his surprise birthday party for the weekend after his birthday which they had planned to keep him off guard. His wife tossed him out, and the group of friends returned the new set of golf clubs they had chipped in to buy.

Gammerman, now back in his old bedroom at his mother's house, refused to allow himself the luxury of regret but returned that first night, and every night thereafter to listen to his mother's lectures on his behavior while the two of them sat in her kitchen eating take-out.

Mixed Messages

Time was all he had left. He knew he had time, but he wanted more no matter how much he had. He thought he could barter his way to more time. Where would he go to do this? Ebay? Farmer's market? The dark web?

He decided to ask his rabbi. She gave him a rabbinical answer which was of no help to him whatsoever. She thought it was and was proud of herself and took the rest of the day off and went bowling with the Methodist minister who was just stopping by to say hello.

They bowled and went to the shore and ate full bellied fried clams, onion rings and drank Birch Beer. Both knew they'd have heartburn.

The minister worried if the rabbi would feel guilty so he told her not to. She told him guilt is one of the only certainties in her life and not to try and take it away from her.

They rode back in silence.

But this is a story about a man and his time, not about people of the cloth. The man, knowing he had time, decided that he didn't have to worry about time this very minute and decided to go to the shore and have some seafood. He saw the rabbi and the Methodist minister take their food on trays out to the outdoor benches in the sunshine. He told the counter person he'd have the same thing they ordered.

That evening he had terrible heartburn from the fried food.

The heartburn turned out to be a heart attack, a fatal one.

He should have kept up his quest for more time the rabbi said at his funeral. The Methodist minister, who was co-captain with the man on his curling team, also gave a eulogy. He said that his friend was in a better place.

If his friend would've heard this, he would have disputed it, but the people in the Synagogue nodded their heads in agreement.

There is a happy ending here but not for the man with the heartburn, but for the rabbi and the Methodist minister who ended up living together, but not marrying because neither would consent to convert.

Only Hope of the Jews

c. 1954 Father Panik Village Projects

You're sitting on your stoop thinking how much you hate the stoop, the building you live in with six side-by-side apartments (now called town houses) and the neighborhood. You hate the neighborhood because all of the stoops in all of the buildings and all of the miniscule wire-fenced-in tiny yards smaller than a jail cell look alike and your fourteen-years-old self can't wait to get out of these projects and scrub the stigma off and live in a place where you don't need the roach exterminator every month and head lice are the main pets for the little kids and on top of it all your family are the only Jews in all the buildings. There are lots of colored's and Puerto Ricans (who are mortal enemies) and plenty of white people and there's a big Catholic Church on the corner across from the corner store and its two pin balls and playing those pinballs are your only solace here.

You look to your left and you see a couple of older and bigger kids coming down the walk and you reach behind you and grab the rock that you scraped against the cement stoop to make jagged edges that makes your fist a weapon and you don't care how big or how many Jew haters there are you will go after them. Rock in hand you'll punch them repeatedly until they subdue you and "teach you a lesson." You know you'll never learn your lesson and when your mother comes home, she'll take one look at you and punish you for fighting and you never tell her you're the only hope of the Jews and she thinks you've gotten to be a ruffian since you had to move to the projects, and that unlike your brother and sisters you're hanging out with the wrong crowd. You take your punishment from her and dream of owning a car and driving as far away from that stoop as you can.

My Tanta Belle Meets Someone's Tanta Miriam at The Supermarket

So, she said come up and visit some time, my Tanta Belle told me in our nightly phone call. We were standing in the produce aisle looking into each other's carts; she said when this woman asked. What gives? You never visit anymore, and you used to visit me all the time. Are you too busy or just too busy with new friends for old friends, and how come you have leeks? What do you do with leeks? I thought they gave you gas she says to me.

I'm not too busy I told her, and would love to visit you, and the leeks are for my neighbor. I've never eaten leeks. She makes leek pancakes and I'm looking forward to trying them but I don't remember any gas problem. So, I asked this woman for her address, and she laughed and said, See it's been so long you can't remember my address.

Next, you'll tell me that you can't remember my name. Won't that be a hoot?

To tell you the truth, I told her, taking a pen and envelope out of my purse, please write down your phone number so I don't forget again, and while you're at it add your name too. Then this woman whom I've never seen before hands me a piece of paper and says, here, you write down your name and number, and call me, and tell me how the leek pancakes were.

White Elephant

Lilly, tired and sad, sits at the card table that doubles as her dining table drumming her fingers on the red and white oilcloth that covers her ripped top card table tablecloth and she looks at the men's and woman's heads solid without features all in red and yellow that is new to her bought from the white elephant sale for a dime really nine pennies she'd scrounged from the bottom of her purse at the grade school sale on the corner yesterday to replace her gray and black animal oil cloth she'd had for several years that she couldn't stand anymore because most of the animals and all of the trees had been picked off while she sat smoking her Pall Malls playing solitaire or listening to the soap operas on her Philco and she couldn't afford to buy a new oil cloth even though hers had animals missing and a story to go with each one she's picked off with her cut and filed but not manicured nails after her programs she'd take out her Ouija Board and ask it if she'd ever find true happiness again or was she destined to be unhappy until the day she died whenever that came and it couldn't be soon enough to get out of this miserable world where all her six sisters were married and had decent factory or office jobs and they were still married and could buy a new oilcloth every year and her eldest two sisters lived out of state and they wrote her often and while they never mentioned it they each put two dollars in their letters each time and Lilly counted on that money for food and to supplement her two part time jobs one as a bookkeeper and the other where she had to take two busses to get to the rabbi's house and cook several meals at a time for him so she only went three days a week and he'd always leave her an envelope with an extra dollar and a note about the food he wanted cooked and at least once a week he also told her in his note that he had bought too much of something and as a favor to him would she take something home because it was a *shanda*, a shame, to waste any of her good cooking so Lilly took, but each time she picked up around his flat and mopped the kitchen floor and since she was hired as a cook she could justify cleaning up and without shame tell her sisters what she cooked for the week in her letters and on her party line tell her more local sisters her news of the day and listen to their rabbi gossip and she sipped from her glass of Manischewitz closed her eyes and put all of her fingers lightly on the planchette and felt it move while asking if tomorrow will finally be a better day and the planchette stopped and Lilly was both hesitant and anxious to open her eyes so she sat still while the wine kicked in and the ash on her cigarette in the ash tray grew longer and she dozed off not seeing that it pointed to *Yes*.

Champ

This was my opportunity to be called "Champ". I liked the idea, the sound of the word, and the way the letters rolled around from tongue to palate. Most "Champs" are boxing champions. This will not be the case with me.

I plan on being the craps champ of Las Vegas. I'm thirty-two and have been rolling the bones since I was a young boy playing Chutes and Ladders. I was good at that and won the nursery school tournament and was called Champ by my classmates.

This time is different. Last month the postcards went out inviting the top twenty craps players to Vegas to compete in the World Craps Competition. I practice rolling the cubes three to four hours a day and my fingers have taken on a longish bent persona much like having shrimp fingers. I would attribute my shrimp fingers to my success because I can grab the dice a certain way and increase my odds of getting the number I'm shooting for. Of course, nothing is guaranteed, but an advantage is an advantage.

Some of the older players have accused me of cheating because of my shrimp fingers but they're only talking jive to try and get me off my game. They all have their signature ways of grabbing and rolling the dice and I don't accuse them of cheating.

I'm scheduled for table 1 with nine others, and our top five get to play their top five for the finals. I show up with my cooler of water so I can keep my shrimp fingers hydrated. We get introduced to the audience but not each other since we all know one another.

We each have our seconds. Mine is my Uncle Morty who spent his army time shooting craps and playing cards. If he sees me acting a little uptight, he'll massage my shoulders, cool me down by waving a towel in my face, and keep me supplied with fresh chilled water and Raisinettes along with marble Halvah.

My table went first and naturally I was in the top five and moving on to the finals table. The favorite of table 2, Bare-Assed Brodsky just squeaked by. It appeared he lost his concentration for a few minutes and according to Vegas Rules he plays in the nude hoping to distract the other players. He's never been Champ but has come in second twice.

We take a break for lunch, and I have my lucky sandwich—chopped liver on raisin bread cut into diagonal quarters and onion rings. Some of the players shared a lunch table but for me it's just me and Uncle Morty. All part of the psych game. The bell rings, we line up around the craps table, take out a roll of bills, exchange them for $1000 and $500 chips and in forty-five minutes it's just me and Bare-Assed Brodsky left. He throws snake eyes and then box cars twice and passes me the dice and I go all in, grab the dice with my shrimp fingers, move them around the table, have Uncle Morty Raisinette and water me and I pick the ivories up, blow on them and roll. Brodsky and I are looking at each other and not at the dice on the felt. There's the collective intake of breath and the cry of Champ followed by applause breaking out.

Still not looking, Brodsky and I turn towards each other and engage in an uncomfortable Bro hug.

Meet My Family

My family is different, wonderful really, but different. They don't ever argue or correct each other. They never say a harsh word to one another or reprimand another's child they just stop speaking to each other for very long periods of time. These quiet times are almost never over real injustices, only perceived ones.

It doesn't take much. A look will do it, or a glance, a raised eyebrow, or a lowered lip. A whisper, nod, point of a finger, a nod and a point, a point and a whisper, nod, and whisper, or especially nod, point, and whisper. Even a shrug, a gesture, a smirk, laugh or eye roll, a tilt of the head, a quizzical look. Or a stare, a twitch, or a yawn. Even a bad meal (you didn't care enough), a meal too good (putting on airs), instant coffee (good enough for this side of the family), frugality (when it comes to us), conspicuous consumption (showing off), a hrrumph, or a too loud belch.

You! Don't worry. They are going to love you. Just be yourself. Don't gush. Sometimes you gush. They hate gush. Me? I think it's adorable personally. No. Never be obsequious, worse than gush. This is not like an inspection it's a simple meeting. Don't worry. If I love you, they will love you. Guaranteed! Don't wring your hands, they will take it as a sign of weakness. No- blasé' is no good, inquisitive is ok if it's not like nosy, not indifferent, or too well dressed or attractive (that's high-falutin'). Not sloppy-they hate sloppy. Just be yourself. Don't hang on to me. Of course I like it! They will say clingy. Don't stay away. Remote and uncaring I can hear them now. Stop worrying.

They will talk about the ones they don't talk to who are not there or even the ones that are there. Trust me on this one. Just nod. Don't let them draw you into agreeing with them because the next thing you'll know they will be talking to each other and not to you. Family. Ah! Family.

How long? The silences usually range from six months to, well sometimes for ever. Things like shrugs, raised eyebrows and the like are usually only six months to a year unless of course during that time a person is shrugged back at and then this could go on indefinitely.

Weddings, bar mitzvahs, anniversaries, holidays have no effect. They all go and look through each other and talk about each other. A funeral. Ahh. Another story altogether. That starts a new slate. There is nothing like a good death to bring my people together. Everybody talks to everybody, and no mention is made of past transgressions.

Oh sure. A new perceived injustice could begin at a funeral. Many do. Perfectly within the rules. Happens all the time. It is very rarely with the same people.

That's part of what makes my family so unique.

OK. Crisis. It depends. Say someone is hospitalized and it's not too serious. They will go but if the parties are not speaking, they will continue not to speak even during the visit. If it is serious, they will speak formally and politely while looking at the other person's forehead or ear. Never eye contact. Just in case, God forbid, of a death, they can say, "Well at least we spoke."

Ready? They are going to love you. Fine. You will be fine. Believe me. I know them like I know the back of my hand. Here, spit out the gum before we go in. It will save on chewing cud comments. Pick up your feet when you walk. No. It doesn't bother me. Not to worry! Don't slouch, they hate slouching and if you can remember to sit up in your chair and not talk with your mouth full this will be a breeze. No, you don't do that. I'm just saying, that's all. Of course. You look terrific! Pay no attention to their remarks about being braless or having long unruly hair. No. It's not how I feel. I love you just the way you are. It is not unruly to me it's natural— the way I like it. Please don't whine. Sobbing. No that's no good either. Why don't we just wait a few minutes while you compose yourself. Whatever got into you? It's only my family.

Audra

Audra is my current girlfriend. She is the rowing coach at a local junior college. For weeks, before she became my girlfriend, I would sit on the grass at lunchtime eating my sandwich and watch her coach. She would pace along the river's edge with a stopwatch and megaphone yelling out instructions to her two racing teams. Before that, I'd been watching her from my office window since I first noticed the sculls on the river and on the first sunny day I took my brown bag down by the water. At first I sat on one of the benches and then, wanting to hear her voice and see her up close, I moved to the crest of the grass overlooking the river.

She walked over and asked me if she could share my sandwich because she hadn't eaten breakfast. Sure, I said, and handed her a half of my Swiss, lettuce, tomato and sprouts on pumpernickel. In between bites she let me know that she knew I'd been watching every day—even the days I pretended to read the book I always carried.

Sometimes I did read my book, but I didn't correct her. As she was leaving that first day, she asked me to bring her a tuna on rye the next, light on the mayo and lots of lettuce. I brought her sandwiches every day after that and one day she ran off without ordering and I showed up the next day with a gas station convenience store ready-made baloney on white, the only thing besides liverwurst that was left. I wouldn't think of eating either one of those, so I got myself a yogurt and a pack of crackers and cheese.

Audra took one bite of her sandwich and gave me a disgusted look before shoving the sandwich back at me and grabbing my yogurt. Jews don't eat that combination of foods; she instructed me using her megaphone from five feet away. I megaphoned my hands and yelled back that who'd know better than me since I wasn't eating anything like it. That night we went out for Chinese.

I was first attracted by her smile (did I mention I kept binoculars in my office?); she smiles often and even though she's tired and I mean sick and tired of hearing this; if you had to describe her in one word it would be adorable. Katie Couric used to go through the same thing when she first came on the Today show.

But best of all, Audra loves to give oral sex. (I have no personal knowledge of Katie Couric in this respect.) Audra often tells me that we were made for each other since I love being on the receiving end. Who am I to argue? Once we were driving by a Chrysler Dealership and she said we should go test-drive a van. She had her head in my lap before we got off the lot. She's such a kidder, always pulling stunts like that. The best was going through the drive-in at McDonald's. I ordered while she went about her business and when we got to the window to pay, she lifted her head and told the teen to make sure the fries were hot and then went back down on me. The kid pulled the fries out of the bag and yelled for someone to bring him new ones. He stood there with a frozen smile pretending that nothing was going on but never taking his eyes off the back of Audra's head, even as he handed me my order.

There's much more to Audra than oral sex, she's bright, witty, and fun to be with. But let's face it, if your girlfriend has to have a fixation, this is a pretty good one to have.

We've been together two years now and there's never been any talk of marriage or living together. It's not that I wouldn't entertain such thoughts, but Audra once told me a joke:

"How do you get a Jewish woman to stop giving blow jobs?"

"I don't know," I played along. "How?"

"Marry her," Audra laughed.

I mean, I'd hate to walk down the aisle and then on our honeymoon have her tell me that she'd given me fair warning and if I'd chosen not to hear it, why is she to blame? Know what I mean?

A Somewhere Diner

Mirsky noticed them right off. They were standing patiently waiting for a table to be cleared when he walked in. He cut the line and took a seat at the counter and a few minutes later the waitress, waving her mop cloth, motioned them to a corner booth directly in his view.

What a view it was. She—about thirty with high, model style cheekbones, big innocent eyes with not so innocent long dark lashes, and henna colored hair hanging long in a planned disheveled look. She wore a black satiny three buttons open blouse, and "watch my wiggle" black jeans with a fire red belt—no rings—no jewelry.

He—naturally curly blond hair, short, pressed pants with suspenders and an Izod striped shirt and Nike sneakers. Spotlessly clean hands and face. Age—about three years.

She didn't look the type to be in this off the highway diner. She neither looked at others nor noticed others looking at her. Good thing. Mirsky couldn't take his eyes off her.

Mirsky knew her. He had never met her, but he knew all about her. The boy too. Mirsky felt he always had the ability to study a person for a few minutes and do a biography. This talent was inherited from walks with his mom when he was young. They invariably would pass someone Mirsky didn't know, but his mother and the passerby would nod their hellos, and as Mirsky, and his mom would continue on, she would give him a short biographical profile with a touch of gossip about that person. *Ann Bigelow, look at her, my goodness! She was voted class sophisticate. No man was ever good enough for her and they were all after her. It was said that she would work all year to save for a cruise hoping to land Mr. Rich. Doesn't look so good for Miss Sophisticate.*

His mom either had a wide circle of acquaintances or a very fertile imagination. Mirsky never knew which.

They were passing through on the way to her mother's house. Probably had about three more hours of driving to go. D.C., maybe

Virginia. No ring. Recently separated or divorced. Poor kid. Mirsky knew what it was like.

They order. His name is probably Brett. Looks like a Brett. Makes his bed every day, and brushes his teeth without being reminded. Short grownup

She sips her cocktail. He tries his Coke. She smiles at Brett. Brett smiles back at Mother.

Brett must call her mother. Mother probably called him Brett honey. Mirsky wonders if Brett will ever slide into third and then decides he would. Looks like a three-year-old winner.

Mother starts on salad. Brett spoons his fruit cocktail.

As noisy as this diner is, Brett and Mother could have been in their own dining room. They look only at their plates, each other, and now together at the main course being served.

Mother and Brett dab with napkins as choreographed.

Mother starts on her scallops. Brett picks up a drumstick.

Kids got an appetite. That isn't even a child's portion of fried chicken.

Mother leaves some scallops.

Brett leaves nothing but picked bones.

Mother and Brett order.

Mother sips her coffee.

Brett starts on the strawberry ice cream.

Well, what do you know? Brett can't even eat half his dessert. The little grownup is rubbing his eyes. Funny, he doesn't seem the type to crawl onto Mother's lap. He looks so cute, and innocent all cuddled up and resting his head against Mother's bosom

Mother sips.

Brett yawns.

Mother touches Brett's head.

Brett unbuttons two buttons on Mother's blouse.

Mother sips.

Brett nurses.

Mother and Brett both close their eyes.

Mirsky almost spills his third cup of coffee.

Then a guy dressed in jeans and a Red Sox baseball cap walks to the counter, blocking Mirsky's view. Finally, stepping aside, he snaps his fingers and gives a whistle for the waitress, who turns and throws him a stare. He, oblivious to her hostility says, "Hey Hon, give me a tuna sandwich and a cup of coffee, black, to go."

Baseball cap turns, and Mirsky watches as Mother opens her eyes at the sound of his whistle. He motions to Mother, who smiles and gently nudges Brett. Mother waves, buttons up, tosses some money on the table, and leads Brett by the hand over to the counter, where she stops and gives baseball cap a hug and a passionate kiss. Picking Brett up, he says, "C'mon son, you can sleep in the car. It's all fixed and we can make Boston by dark." He hands his to-go order to Mother and they leave. Go figure, Mirsky thinks. Grabbing his check, he waits his turn for the cashier, and realizes there is something familiar about her, kind of a Midwest preacher's daughter look. Mirsky figures her name to be Rachel or Rebecca, and that she's working here to support her child born out of wedlock. She can't go home because of the scandal it would cause her parents.

Mirsky pays the bill and looks at her nametag, Tami. Poor kid, Mirsky thinks, had to change her name too. He shakes his head as he leaves the restaurant.

Me and Zeyde

I am the bald man on the left of the picture, or I could be. He is my Zeyde, Isaac "Ike" at approximately seventy-three, the age I am now. Maybe he's a few years older, but not many.

I am the young man on the right, home for a visit after four years in the Air Force and two in California where I was an Air Traffic Controller. Zeyde does not understand when I tell him I get paid to talk to airplanes. He smiles as if I'm teasing him.

I didn't have any children yet when this picture was taken. I was twenty-six, married a year, and used to understand my Zeyde better when he spoke Yiddish to me. Now, from lack of use, I miss some words. I speak English back to him and he gets the majority, I'm pretty sure.

Both my children are in their forties now. Zeyde lived to be eighty-eight. I would like a picture of myself with some of my grandchildren sitting with me and me looking as content and happy as Zeyde.

Little things appealed to him: a shot of schnapps (any liquor from Scotch to Crème de Menthe was Schnapps to him), or a meal where he could suck the marrow from the bones. I liked that too and at times he'd hand me the bone and watch me work at getting the marrow out. A walk after a meal followed by a nap lying down in the grass or anywhere, he wasn't fussy. I like my naps too and my schnapps.

Zeyde was a carpenter and taught me a lot and allowed me to work with him summers and weekends. He told me he was still working but no more big jobs. He talked about when he was starting out on his own, he'd ride his bike to work, carrying lumber on one shoulder and holding his tool box and handlebar with his other hand. He always stopped at the lumberyard where he knew everyone, put things on his bill, and ride off to work, miles most days. If he needed any more, he'd come back at lunch but would never leave any extra lumber on site for fear of having it stolen. He looked so proud the day I told him I wanted to be a carpenter like him.

People thought he was illiterate because he spoke with an accent. Every day he read *The Forward*, a Jewish newspaper written in Yiddish. He could also read Hebrew, write and speak Polish, Russian, as well as English and of course Yiddish. Not bad for a man with only a few years of education.

My grandmother died when I was four or five and while I was in the service he remarried. He was pursued by a three-time widow who wanted a man with his own house. Most of his children did not like her but she was always nice to me, and Zeyde was content.

In the picture, I like how I have my arm pressed against his back and he has a hand on my leg.

We used to watch wrestling together on TV and once, when I was sitting on the floor and he in his chair swearing in Yiddish at the bad guy, he sprung off the chair and pinned me before he realized what he did. That was during his six-foot, pot-bellied days. He's not six feet in this picture and doesn't have a pot belly but he still liked his schnapps, a good meal, a walk afterwards and a nice nap.

Conversion

I married a robot. My family wouldn't come to the wedding because she wasn't Jewish. They sat Shiva for a week. The whole meshuggah nine yards; torn black ribbons, covered mirrors, cushions off the chairs, pastrami, corned beef, and tuna sandwiches on seeded rye. Coffee cakes.

She decided to convert eight months after the wedding and took the name Freya. She then went to the mikvah. Unfortunately, Freya rusted, which the Rabbi declared voided her conversion so she couldn't be buried in a Jewish Cemetery.

I sat Shiva for her for two days. My family all came. Again, the whole meshuggah nine yards; torn black ribbons, covered mirrors. I had mother call the delicatessen. For 30 people, she said, your #4 Shiva Special; pastrami, corned beef, and tuna sandwiches on seeded rye, but add egg salad this time. Okay, a #5 then. And fresh coffee cakes—don't forget the coffee cakes.

Shabbos Goy

This rabbi of my youth, who shall be nameless, not for his protection, but because I swore to myself that I would never utter his name again, called me into his office one Saturday morning. He was tall and powerful looking, with a scraggly beard that I heard some women say made him look younger instead of more mature. In this Orthodox Shul, when only those saying Kaddish stood or even remained in the Shul, the Rabbi would leave the bema during this prayer. His parents were still living and he used this time to take a break from leading the services. This is when he called me in.

His office was right off the sanctuary, across from the bema. It was very small and windowless, and the walls showed leak marks. His smell was the smell of the room and I felt a little nauseous as I always did when I had to be in his office. The Rabbi's desk was neat with only a pad and the bottom of a milk carton full of pens and pencils. The floor was littered with books and papers, and there was room left only for the two wooden slatted folding chairs that faced his desk.

I had spent the service sitting against the back wall, next to the bema on the opposite side of his office doing "the pages." This was a duty of the twelve-year olds of the congregation. It was a way for the congregation to know which page of the prayer book was being read from. By pulling strings on a box with three slots about twelve feet off the floor the page numbers could be changed. If I was slow in a page change or was daydreaming, the Rabbi would lean over the railing, smiling, as if to tell me something nice. "The page, Shmendrik, change the page."

"Sit down," the rabbi said once I was in his office. I'd been there many times before, too many, and not once had he asked me to sit. Knees knocking, I sat.

"Reuven, I want you to go to my house and do something for my wife." He took off his glasses, fogged them with his breath, and wiped them with his handkerchief. He had never called me by my first name before. I always believed that he thought I only had one name—Mirsky.

"Sure, Rabbi. What would you like me to do?"

"I want you to light the gas stove for her."

I noticed his frayed white shirt as he took off his tallis and hung it up. He sat down. His collar was dirty, too. I saw the rabbi had a bunch of long black hairs growing out of his ears, and his scraggly beard looked knotted up and I thought that maybe his house didn't have a tub. He seemed even taller in his office.

"It's Shabbos, Rabbi. What about Mr. Farley?" I asked.

Mr. Farley was the owner of a small variety store across the street from our Shul. He was the person who would always turn on or off the lights on Shabbos. He was our Shabbos Goy, and was relied on heavily. In fact, if he didn't unlock the door, no one else would. Turning on lights, locking doors, any manual labor was not permitted, so we relied on Mr. Farley.

"Mr. Farley is ill today," the rabbi said with a hint of exasperation in his voice. "The first time in over twenty-five years he can't do his duties. And to think, just last month the congregation presented him with a special "Shabbos Goy Plaque" at a Sunday Men's Club Brunch. But today, even from his sick bed, he came and opened the Shul, turned on the lights, and only then went home. I would have had him do it, but he can't, and my wife, who, as you and every one else knows, is a little scatterbrained, forgot to light the stove before sundown yesterday. So I need someone to do this and I'm sending you."

"Why can't it wait until sundown today, Rabbi?"

Rising from his chair and leaning over his desk glaring at me, he said, "Don't question me. Go to my house."

"But it's a sin, Rabbi. I don't want to sin." I stood in my hand-me-down blue serge suit, hands in coat pockets, shuffling my feet, looking directly at the rabbi.

"Who are you to tell a rabbi what is and what isn't a sin, you little pisher? If I tell you it's okay to do something than it's not a sin. Understand?"

"No."

"Go now, Mirsky," he yelled. "Do you need more trouble than you already have in this world?"

I was looking down at my scuffed shoes, realizing I was getting into trouble and turned red. Not moving, I said, "Why doesn't your wife light the oven, Rabbi?"

"Shame on you for questioning me and mentioning my wife."

"But . . ."

"If you don't do this, Reuven, I'll tell your mother that you don't know your Hebrew well enough to have a Saturday Bar-Mitzvah. Remember, you don't pay dues here." The rabbi looked satisfied with himself. "You'll do your Haftorah on a Monday when all of your friends are in school. Do we understand each other?"

He had me do other things in the past because we were poor and couldn't afford the dues. "Charity cases have to put up with a lot," the rabbi had told me more than once. "It's your way of repaying the Shul. You just can't take, take, take. You must do some giving," he said, more than once.

My mother, like every other woman in the congregation, loved the rabbi. He was young, solicitous, and seemed very wise, especially when he was counseling either an adult or a family. But with the rebbetzin it was a different story. She and the rabbi never walked together, she always walked or stood behind him and I often heard him call her a klutz and make fun of her to others while she stood there. When she lost the last baby, she didn't come to Shul for a month. The rabbi said she felt ashamed for stumbling down the basement stairs and having to stay in the hospital for almost a week. He told his congregants that she had miscarried and to please let her be and not visit her. This made the women love him more and gossip about his wife being a burden on such a fine young man. It was not unusual for him to be invited for dinner at a congregant's house and not bring his wife along.

So, I cleaned the benches, waxed the Ark, picked up papers around the Shul and did what no one else wanted to do. But this was different. I didn't understand why the rabbi's wife wasn't in Shul and sitting in the balcony with the other women, and why she needed the oven turned on during Shabbos.

The rabbi got up, put on his tallis, and returned to the bema.

I slowly walked to the rabbi's house kicking stones ahead of me. I rang the bell and the rabbi's wife opened the door a crack and in the dark I could only see her in shadow. She said hurriedly, "Go around to the back door."

She let me in, and without looking at me, pointed to the stove. "I forgot to light it before Shabbos," she mumbled. Holding a broom, she stood by the wall as if she was trying to become one with it. I took a wooden match from the box and lit the pilot lights on the burners.

"They're lit," I told her, sneaking a glance her way. Her wig was slightly off center, and she turned away from me, but not before I saw her face was bruised on one side. Her lip hung down and her cheek was swollen.

She saw me peeking and moved back deeper into the shadows. "Oven too," she mumbled. "I forgot that, too."

Getting down on my knees in my Shul clothes, I opened the bottom door and lit the oven pilot light. As I was brushing off my knees, I saw the counter with peeled potatoes and carrots, and several chickens lying on a board next to the sink.

"Go," she said.

"Mirsky," I said, and ran out of the house heading back to Shul.

She must have had another fall and didn't feel up to it today. Cooking is one thing, but cleaning? My Mother did her cleaning always the day before and we had our Shabbos meal on Friday nights after she lit the candles at sunset.

As with many of the women, my mother left Shul after the first service, not waiting for the second. She would go home and prepare a cold lunch—sandwiches, borscht, and whatever leftovers she could serve from the night before. It would be waiting for my brothers and me when we got home, after we changed clothes.

Leaving the rabbi's house running, I rounded the corner one block from Shul and had to stop before slamming into a group of women. They had the sidewalk blocked and I couldn't cut into the street and go around them because of the parked cars. I could hear them jabbering away as I stopped.

"What are you doing out of Shul?" my mother asked moving to the front of the group. The other ladies stood behind my mother and said nothing.

"I was on an errand for the rabbi," I told her.

"On Shabbos? The rabbi sent you on an errand? Hah!" my mother said. The other women whispered to each other and shook their heads. "And did this errand cause you to get your Shabbos clothes dirty?"

"Yes," I said. "I have to go back to Shul now."

"Oh, *now* you want to go to Shul. Where have you been, tell me?"

"I told you, Mom."

Surrounded by the women who had crept up around my mother, her lips quivering as they do when she's really angry, she asked in a very controlled voice, "And what was this errand for our rabbi that was so important as to take you out of Shul?"

"He sent me to his house," I said.

"His house?"

"Yes."

"Why did the rabbi send you to his house?" my mother asked.

"He needed me to do something for the rebbetzin," I said.

"What?" she demanded.

I looked down at the sidewalk and pushed a pebble around with my shoe.

"Well?" she demanded.

"To light the oven for the rebbetzin." I confessed.

"Light the oven on Shabbos? You are going to stand there and tell me that you are taking Mr. Farley's place as the Shul's new Shabbos Goy?" my mother asked, raising both hands to her heart.

I stared at her, knowing that there was no right answer.

The women, some with hands covering their mouths, looked unbelieving and angry.

Her slap across my face sent me into the bushes, where a hole was ripped in my suit coat. Tears welled in my mother's eyes. "Liar! Wait till I get you home!"

I got up and took off running. At the corner I turned around to see if she was chasing me. She wasn't. All the other women talked and continued as one, but my mother, handkerchief in hand, stood alone waiting for the light to change so she could cross to the other side of the street.

It was after dark when I finally succumbed to hunger and fatigue and went home to get "what was coming" to me. I immediately went up to the bedroom I shared with my older brother, Herby and changed out of my Shabbos suit, into dungarees and a polo shirt. Shelley, my younger brother, wasn't there. I walked slowly down the stairs and into the kitchen, passing the living room where my mother sat, head in her hands, talking on the phone. Herby looked up from his book and smiled and did a neck slash with his finger. He had probably been waiting hours for me to come home to get my beating. There was a plate on the table with a drumstick, a baked potato, and a mixture of peas and carrots. It wasn't hot or cold, but I ate it down quickly and opened the refrigerator looking for dessert. I took out a small glass bowl of red Jello, and ate it standing. Feeling fortified, I went into the living room and sat down on the couch. I could feel its springs pushing into my legs.

"Do you have any idea how much you shamed me in front of the other women?" My mother grabbed a fistful of her hair in each hand. Her face was red and wet, her knuckles white.

"Mom. Please don't cry."

"I won't punish you if you tell the truth," she lied.

"This time you should tell Mom the truth," Herby smiled.

"I did. Why don't you mind your own business?"

She said, "That was Mrs. Levine on the phone, who spoke to Mrs. Cutler, who mentioned to the rabbi our running into you coming back from his house. The rabbi said he didn't know what she was talking about."

"There's got to be a mistake, Mom. Geez, that's what happened," I said.

"He's calling the rabbi a liar, Mom." Herby was smiling.

"I wish God would take me," my mother pleaded. "I can't handle this anymore. I can't face my neighbors and certainly not the rabbi." Mom always knew that her wishing for death was the sure fire way to bring out the truth and apologies.

I said nothing. Herby smirked at me when Mom wasn't looking. I was going to get a beating and my brother put down his book to watch.

"Well?" Mom asked.

"Tell Herby to stop smirking at me," I said.

Herby had the book back up by the time my mother turned towards him.

"Don't change the subject. I asked you a question."

I said nothing.

Mom turned her back and hung her head. "Where did I go wrong? I tried my best to raise you as good, decent kids and what do I get? I get a son who has no shame and can lie with a straight face. I wish I were dead."

"Mom. Don't say that," Herby said, running over to Mom hugging her. "We need you. Don't wish that."

I didn't cry. Herby crossed his eyes at me.

"Other mothers believe their kids." Kicking the couch until my foot hurt, I said, "I don't care about a Bar Mitzvah anymore." Stomping out of the room, I wished that my mother would die.

I had my Bar Mitzvah on a Monday with none of my friends there—only a bunch of old men smelling of snuff, my mother, grandfather, my brothers Herby, and Shelly. Herby didn't want to take off from school, but Mom made him take a half-day. Shelley was too young for school. I chanted my Hebrew but didn't make a speech. After the service there was a bottle of Four Roses brought by my grandfather, a decanter of wine, and some cookies and strudel my mother baked. I got no presents.

I never got to stand on a chair, after the blessing over the challah and the wine, with all of my friends surrounding me as I tossed out chocolate bars from a box. I had watched all of my friends do that and always got caught up in the excitement of trying to catch more than one and watching the Bar Mitzvah boy toss extra Hershey Bars towards his closest friends and try to keep them from the kids he really didn't like. Standing on the chair tossing out chocolates was the culmination of the ceremony—the part where everyone looked up to you. On my Bar Mitzvah Day no one looked up to me.

My grandfather shook my hand as did many of the old timers in the Shul, and they drank shots of Four Roses and ate my mother's strudel and cookies.

The Bar Mitzvah ceremony for my own son, Eric, was wonderful. His chanting was the sweet chanting of a voice not yet changed. My wife, Elaine, and I held hands as we walked to the Bema. Together we started our Aliyah, but I choked up and Elaine finished for both of us. Before we knew it the ceremony was over and we were heading to the social hall for the prayers over the bread and wine. Herby said the Motze over the challah, and Shelley said the prayer for the wine.

Herby got drunk at Eric's Bar Mitzvah. We sat together and drank shots of peppermint schnapps and made silly toasts.

"I keep remembering," Herby said, pouring two more shots, "When you were Eric's age and got in all that trouble with Mom and the rabbi . . ."

"Herby, I don't want to think about that, much less talk about it," I said.

"When I saw you walk out of Shul that day I followed you to the rabbi's house. I was watching through the window when you lit the rebbetzin's oven." He laughed, and then burped. "Gotcha good on that one. Mom was so busy tracking you that I could do anything I wanted without getting into trouble. And let me tell you—I did plenty."

I stood and turned away from Herby and wandered back into the sanctuary. At the wall of memorial plaques, I stared at my mother's plaque. "Now you know the truth," I said, trying not to hear her calling me a liar.

Herby came up from behind and clapped me on the shoulder. He touched two fingers to our mother's plaque and then to his lips. "You should forgive him now, Mom, he's straightened himself out." He smirked at me and went back to the party. I started to say something else to my mother, but realized there was nothing left to say.

Zvi A. Sesling

For my wife Susan J. Dechter, who keeps our Jewish lives grounded. And thank you to the editors and publications that published some of these stories in which all the characters are fictional and any resemblance to those living or dead is purely coincidental.

Festival of Lights

Jacob Schnitzel is about seven when it happens. His mother and father invite four couples for the last night of Hanukkah. They open the dining table so it can seat the extra people. Then they add folding chairs to accommodate eveyone. They place two overlapping paper tablecloths on the extended table and Mrs. Schnitzel tells her husband Mendel to put out the best dishes, the China ones with the matching sterling silver utensils. "We wouldn't want the Friedmans, Gelmans, Shapiros or Karps to think we are poor."

"Well, they know we aren't, that's why I bought that Cadillac to drive around in. It's why I keep it out on the street during the day," Mendel says.

Next they place their large *Hanukkiah* with nine candles on the table. Sophie Schnitzel then goes to the kitchen to prepare the *latkes.* She shreds the potatoes, adds salt and pepper, a little flour and then puts some vegetable oil in two frying pans and begins cooking.

For the Schnitzel family this is one of the two big social events of the year, the other being Passover when they host the first night with all its trappings and the home cooked meal that Sophie spends preparing the entire day. Then the Friedmans, Gelmans, Shapiros and Karps each host one night of gustatorial evenings with the remaining two nights seeing each family eating in their own home.

Shortly before four the couples arrive. Sumner and Alice Friedman enter first. Then Max and Sarah Gelman followed by Julius and Sadie Shapiro and finally David and Louise Karp. They are all invited to join the Schnitsels in a glass of Mogen David Concord Grape Wine and some cream cheese and lox on crackers. Sumner Friedman wants to discuss politics, but the others reject him, preferring to talk about the latest movies. Julius Shapiro prevails by insisting on talking about sports, while the women discuss how wonderfully their children are doing in school. The social hour continues until the bottle of Mogen David Concord Grape Wine and the crackers are finished.

"Well," Mendel Schnitzel says, "let's adjourn to the dining room if the dinner is ready." He looks to Sophie who nods an affirmative.

Mendel leads the procession to the dining room table and directs each couple to their chairs. When they all sit, Mendel leads everyone in prayer and songs.

Sophie heads for the kitchen, followed by Mendel. A few minutes later she brings out the latkes on a large tray, three heaping plates full of the well-done evening meal while Mendel follows with a tray filled with dishes of apple sauce and sour cream, cooked green beans and carrots.

Carefully, Sophie lights the *Shamus*, the Head Candle, then with the *Shamus* she lights the rest from right to left. Everyone sings two more Hanukkah songs.

Finally, Mendel says, "It's time for dinner, but before let us be seated and say a prayer for this holiday feast.

"And don't forget we each must say what Hanukkah means to us," Sophie adds.

However, as they finish saying a prayer and before the meaning of the holiday can be discussed, young Jacob stretches halfway across the table as he reaches out for one of the potato pancakes which Sophie has stacked neatly. As he does he slips a bit in his chair, his outstretched arm knocking over the *Hanukkiah* and all the lighted candles.

Almost immediately the paper tablecloths catch fire, flames crawling across the table as the guests first grab the food and then the plates and utensils. Everyone waves their hands and yells, confusion reigns and as they all head in different directions with the plates, utensils and food, Sophie points to the coffee table and orders everyone at the top of her lungs to put everything down on the table in front the sofa.

In the confusion of burning tablecloths, food, dinnerware and utensils being saved and moved and yelling while trying to put out the flames one of the guests pushes the burning paper tablecloths to the floor where the now flaming paper's blaze leaps to the drapes, the conflagration reaches upward toward the ceiling.

Everyone is in full panic mode. Sophie and Alice gather the dishes while Sumner and Max grab the silverware. David tries to pick up the *Hanukkiah* but it burns his hand and he drops it causing more of the paper tablecloth to catch fire. Sarah, Sadie and Louise grab pillows off the sofa to try and beat down the flames. Everyone rushes around chaotically while Sophie yells "Oy, Oy vay!" They are all escalating the panic except Mendel who makes a dash to the kitchen, fills a pail with water from the sink. He races back to where the flames make their way upward..

Suddenly, all the commotion stops, each person frozen in place. Then panic erupts again. The Friedmans and the Gelmans make their way to the front door, while the Shapiros run around the room yelling to call the fire department while the Karps say to call the police. It is, Mendel, however, who returns from the kitchen with the pail, aims carefully and tosses the aqueous contents on the impending inferno. He repeats his heroic run to the kitchen, filling the pail once again and returning to extinguish what remains of the burning fragments.

They all reenter the dining room where the guests stomp on the now dying embers which fall to the floor and assure each other it is really safe to remain in the Schnitzel residence.

After they convince themselves of their safety, Sophie and the women get the food, dishes and silverware back on the table, minus the paper tablecloths and the drapes. The men bring in the food from the kitchen. They open all the windows to let out the smoke and odor, then after the quick cleanup everyone finally sits down to a smoky dinner.

Everyone except Jacob who is sent to his room with no dinner.

Holy Day

Our synagogue, B'nai Etz, sits at the east corner of our town, a solitary building not near any other because it is a Jewish edifice in a predominantly Christian community. Everyone seems to get along well, though occasionally there is a fight, not a gang fight because we have no gangs. However, once in a while a group of Christian teens cross paths with Jewish teens, trade a few insults and settle it with fisticuffs. Neither side wins or loses, but everyone has a few cuts and bruises or maybe black eyes. Sometimes there is a broken nose or some torn clothes. Never is there a weapon and except for that occasional nose, no broken bones. The boys tell their parents they fell off their bike.

The next day the same young men who a day earlier had battled would find themselves on the same football or baseball team for their high school, Alexander Hamilton.

Of the three of us, Herbie Tanner, Andy Feiner and me, Ernie Goldman, Andy is the biggest, nearly six foot, three inches tall and weighing two hundred and thirty pounds, so he plays right tackle and fullback on the Hamilton Federals. Herbie is the smallest at five-ten, one hundred and sixty-five pounds. I am in the middle at six foot even and one hundred and ninety pounds. We call ourselves the Three Musketeers even though we had no muskets or any other weapon for that matter.

We always hang out together, triple date in my car, an Oldsmobile Ninety-Eight and sit together at lunch break. We take as many courses together as we can. With my poor math ability I am in a lower class than Andy and Herbie. We always sit together in study hall which gets us in trouble because during study hall no one is supposed to communicate with anyone else.

So one afternoon Andy wants Herbie and me to meet him. He writes a note in Hebrew but uses English lettering. When he finishes he folds it neatly into a little square and goes to pass it over to me except Miss King intercepts it. She unfolds the square Andy has neatly folded and looks at it.

"So, what are you two up to?" she asks sternly.

"It's our Hebrew School homework," I say confidently figuring she will never know the difference and let us continue our correspondence.

Miss King studies it for a minute and then shifts her head from me to Andy and back to me. "So, if that's true why does it say, *Meet me at the drug store after school?*"

I could feel the heat rise to my cheeks and I imagine Miss King sees the pink flush and looks to Andy who turns to face the windows on the other side of the room.

"Ah, huh. Guess you two will be meeting again after school in this same room, but different seats. Since I will be monitoring detention today I do not expect you two to try anymore of your shenanigans," Miss King tells us.

I can hear some snickers from the other students as Miss King raises her voice for the reprimand. Andy and I both slouch down in the chairs at our desks. We flash a quick glance at each other and put our heads down. I pretend to do homework and I am sure Andy does the same even though I do not dare glance in his direction.

In study hall detention, Andy sits at the front of the room in the first row next to the windows and I sit in the back row on the other side of the room. When detention ends I sarcastically tell Miss King to have a good evening and she ignores me. Andy and I meet outside the room and walk to the drug store where Herbie waits for us at the soda fountain.

"Geeze, I've had three Cokes, a brownie and a Three Musketeers. Where you guys been?"

"Detention," I say coldly.

"That Miss King, a real beaut, caught Andy and me passing a note I wrote in Hebrew with English letters. How was I to know she could read it as well? Nailed us right there with that damn hour and a half detention. So here we are, late but here."

Herbie chuckles and Andy shoots him an angry glare so that he stops mid-chuckle and says, "Sheesh, who'd ever think…"

"Don't matter no more," I say. "Besides, tomorrow is *Rosh HaShanah* and we gotta be in the synagogue by nine."

"And home before five today," Herbie adds.

The next morning, under my mother's strict instructions and supervision, I pick a white-on-white shirt, blue suit, a red tie and polished black shoes. I put my *kippah* in the inside pocket of my suit jacket and go downstairs to eat breakfast. To assure I do not get any food on my clothing, mother has me wear an apron.

The fact is, mother makes nothing that can spill on me, even made me eat my Cheerios without milk and only a glass of water for liquid.

After breakfast we get into Dad's new Buick Roadmaster, a giant of a car in which Andy, Herbie and me triple date. If we are alone, Anita and I stretch our bodies and make out.

When we get to the synagogue Dad parks at the far end so that only one car can park next to him as he does not want any dents or scratches in the new Buick.

We go in and the first half of the service is as it always is all the years I attend. The rabbi takes his usual break, probably the only rabbi who does so my father says, but it is for a good ten minutes.

Andy, Herbie and I decide to go out and have a smoke, which, of course, is against all the rules of the Holy Day, but being eighteen-years-old we think the rule is ridiculous. Besides everyone else is inside and our parents will never admit *their* sons would do such a thing.

As soon as we are outside we scoot around the corner to light up. However, there are four teenage boys with a bucket each of red and black paint, each of them with a brush in their hand painting a swastika on the side of the synagogue.

Andy throws his cigarette on the ground and crushes it with his shoe. Herbie and I do too.

Andy says, "I'll take those two big guys, you guys each get one of the other two."

Before we can make a move Andy silently charges the two bigger guys, arms spread and going full Andy speed wraps his arms around them and slams them to the ground like a pro linebacker.

Herbie and I are behind him, each of us grabbing one of the other two swastika painters. Each of the boys has a brush, one with the bucket of black paint and the other with the bucket of red paint. I hit my target low, gripping him around the shins and forcing him to lose balance and let go of the red paint which spills on my suit, shirt and tie. I really do not think of the paint at the moment as my fists flail away at his face, hitting him in the eyes, cheeks and on the nose, which immediately spurts blood. He has no time to yell or fight back as I grab him by the hair and bang his head into the ground, take the paint brush and swipe it across his face so that it all looks like a bloody mess. I ram my knee into his stomach. He is winded and gasping for air which lets me whack his face a few more times knocking out a couple teeth and causing blood from his lips to merge with the blood streaming from his nose.

Herbie goes shoulder first into his target, knocking him over and then kicks him in the head, face, stomach and groin. He jumps on the kid and begins rubbing his target's face in the black paint and dirt. Then he jumps up and kicks some more as the kid groans and cries.

Andy, in the meantime, has both of the bigger boys in headlocks, one under each of his arms. He bashes their head together, three or four times, lets them fall to the ground and then slams a shoe into each of their faces, twisting his foot to break their noses. As we are causing them more pain a police car arrives and two officers exit, running over to us.

"Hey, hey, what's going on here," says an overweight police sergeant whose partner has a hand on his billy club. I recognize them. One is Irish; the other Italian. The Irish sergeant has that serious police versus criminals look. The other officer stands behind the sergeant. Both of them know Andy, a high school football hero.

Andy points at the wall of the synagogue, "We found these guys painting the swastika and jumped them."

"Yeah," I add, "today is Rosh HaShanah, our New Year and one of our three holiest days. These bastards think they're Nazis or something."

"Yeah," Herbie adds, "they're desecrating our synagogue on a very holy day. Arrest them will you."

The sergeant looks down at the four boys, then at us. He pulls the other officer aside and whispers something. The other officer nods affirmatively. The sergeant walks back to Andy, Herbie and me and says "We're on patrol and need to check out the rest of the area. When we get back we don't expect to see you three here, understand?"

We nod enthusiastically and when the police leave we kick each of the four in the head, ribs, stomach and groin, then head home. Andy's and Herbie's clothes are soiled with dirt and grass stains. My suit, shirt and tie are splattered with red paint. I will have to face my mother but hope when the truth comes out she will forgive me.

Handshake

The first time Herman Milstein sees her he knows he has to ask her out. Carla Gianni is dark, sunflower black eyes and a body that could flatten an entire U.S. Army battalion. Even at sixteen Herman knows she is special though she is only fifteen.

None of his friends ask her out because she is, as they say, darker than a sunburn. Pretty, yes, but too dark. Herman does not care and when he asks her if she would like to get a hamburger at Snooky's, she quickly accepts.

After their second date Carla's father calls Herman's father and says, "I don't like your son dating my daughter because you guys aren't Catholic."

"Good," says Herman's father, "I don't like your daughter dating my son because she's not Jewish."

There is a moment of silene, then Mr. Gianni says, "You know, you and I might get along. Why don't you meet me in my office Thursday, say noon, for lunch. I own Napoli, the restaurant in Little Italy. Noon."

Mr. Milstein is still holding the phone a few seconds later when he realizes Carla's father has hung up and tomorrow is Thursday.

Noon the next day Jacob Milstein arrives at the Napoli. It appears empty but he tries the door anyway which opens so he enters. Four linebacker-looking men greet him and when Jacob says he is there to meet Mr. Gianni two of them pat him down for weapons and two escort him into a private back room where Dominic Gianni is seated behind a round table that is set for two lunches. Dominic rises to greet his guest.

"Dominic Gianni, but most people call me Don."

"Jacob Milstein, but most people call me Jake."

The host orders a meal for two and says, "No pork for you, Jews don't eat it huh?"

No, but the chicken cacciatore is perfect, thank you."

"Glad you like it."

After lunch the two men discuss a plan to keep their children apart and after agreeing Dominic asks "So tell me Jake, what exactly do you do?"

"Well, since we're being so candid and honest with each other, what I do is purchase ammunition, weapons, tanks, any kind of military equipment for the Israeli Army."

"Wow, we having something in common," Dominic says to Jake's raised eyebrows. "The feds would lock us both for a couple decades if they knew what we are doing. God knows they've tried with me, but I got great lawyers. The best."

Jake smiles, "Yeah, I have a great cover. You have this restaurant and I must say the food is superb and I am principal of a Hebrew school."

They both laugh.

"So, you need weaponry for Israel. I like you Jews, you kicked the Brits out and whipped the Arabs solidly. I like that kind of guts."

Jake nods and is about to say something, but Dominic says, "You know I got a ship load of weapons, ammo, tanks, grenades, all kinds of crap on a ship at a Brooklyn pier. There's a bunch of African rebels who'll pay eight hundred thousand for the boat load. For a million it can be in Israel in couple weeks."

Three days later Jake is at the pier in Brooklyn with two large suitcases filled with twenty dollar and hundred dollar bills. Jake hands the suitcases to Dominic who signals the ship to depart. The two men shake hands, a match made in war and crime.

Homeless Man

The homeless man, a Vietnam Veteran, sits on the stairs of the Arlington Street Church. He is dressed in a combat camouflage outfit and wears a green beret. He sits holding another beret into which people drop money because he as a sign leaning against his knees that states, *Homeless, need money for food.*

So I stop and ask, "Would you like money or food?"

"Food," he answers.

"I'll take you to the restaurant next door," I say, pointing to The Public Garden Restaurant, a popular upscale eatery on Arlington Street.

"Can't go there, I been booted outta there twice by the manager. Wouldn't even give me a glass of water."

I am outraged, here I am teaching a course on the history of the Vietmam War and a vet is being denied even a drink of water. I grab his arm and say, "Come on, we're going in there."

"They'll kick us both out," he says.

We walk the few feet to the door and go in. Sure enough as the homeless man predicted the manager comes over and tells the homeless man to leave. "I told you we don't want you homeless people in here. We are a class operation."

My anger is clear as I say, "Look fella, my money is good and this fellow is a hungry veteran who fought in Vietnam and deserves respect."

"Yeah, I bet you'd say that about Holocaust survivors too," the manager says.

"Damn right," I can feel my face getting red. "My parents survived a concentration camp and I try to help our homeless vets."

"Yeah, bet you're on of those do-goody liberals at the college around the corner."

"Yup, you got that right. I work at the newspaper and double as an adjunct teaching the history of the war. I just happen to be a bit more fortunate than this man."

The manager grunts and says, "Well, as long as you have the cash." He turns and leaves, walks toward the kitchen..

After the two of us eat a hearty lunch I walk him back to the church stairs where he takes his place, the sign leaning against his knees, the beret with a couple dollars in his hand."

"Thanks for the lunch," he says, "and sorry your parents had to suffer like that. My parents never did, they were here."

I nod and begin walking toward the subway.

Migration

The last pogrom does it for father who leaves Russia where the dead litter his village. Jewish dead under the guns of the Cossacks.

He says his goodbyes then walks across Eastern Europe and China often hungry and weak, yet never gives up. Somehow he gets a horse and rides it to Turkey. He trades the horse for a hot meal and a jacket and moves on to Syria. Back on foot he walks to Lebanon.

With only his feet carrying him in shoes worn bare he arrives in Israel (then Palestine). He left Russia at age fifteen in 1911 often having to fight his way to survive on his solo journey. He learns Arabic and arrives at his destination in 1912, to survive with inner strength when others do not.

In 1933 mother leaves Prussia, her city becomes part of Germany and after World War II is annexed by the USSR. Her family's persecution is different—Jews rounded up like cattle suffer in death camps. So many on mother's side, perhaps two-thirds of the pre-WWII family murdered by the Nazis. In Russia, father's family either freezes or the Nazis murder them.

Borders changed frequently those days. Father's brothers—two say they are from Russia, father says he is from Lithuania and the youngest brother counts Belarus as the country of his birth. They were all born in the same town. None dare go back. Mother could not bear to see Germany or her hometown now Kaliningrad, Russia.

Everyone has everything stolen from them by the Nazis or the Soviets. Both my parents have to leave their homes, families and friends with only their clothes and shoes. Father meets mother in Israel raises a family in America hoping to be free of fear, but never quite able to forget.

Poor Bernie

The phone wakes Herman Milstein from a sound sleep. He is dreaming about Carla Gianni a girl he meets his junior year in high school when he lives in the Bronx. After two dates nothing comes of it.

Now he is a junior at Boston University and lives in a studio apartment on Babcock Street in Brookline, MA just a block from the business district of Coolidge Corner.

"Hullo," he says in a still drowsy voice.

"Herman, it's your father."

Shaking his head to get rid of the sleep, he answers, "Hi, Dad, what's up for you to call so early?"

"You have classes today?"

"Not 'til my three to five p.m. class."

"Good, it's seven a.m., I'll see you in an hour at Smiley's Nook in Brookline for breakfast."

"And that's all there is to it. You simply take the 10 a.m. shuttle to LaGuardia and Bernie Katz will meet you at the gate. Hand him the suitcase and take the 10:30 shuttle back to Logan. Here's a couple hundred dollars for a cab to Logan, the shuttle tickets and a cab from Logan to your apartment."

Herman asks no questions, takes the suitcase and leaves Smiley's Nook. Outside he hails a cab and sets out for Logan Airport.

The shuttle arrives in LaGuardia in under an hour and when Herman gets to the gate Bernie is there waiting with his usual smile. Herman hands him the suitcase and makes his way back to the return shuttle.

The next day the phone again wakes Herman very early. As he picks up the phone Herman can hear his father calling his name.

"Yeah, I'm here," Herman says, more annoyed that sleepy.

"Herman did you do as I asked you to do yesterday? Did you take the shuttle to La Guardia?"

"Yeah."

"Did Bernie Katz meet you at the gate?"

"Yeah."

"Did you hand Bernie Katz the suitcase? It had a lot of money in it."

"Yeah, then I went back to the shuttle and flew home."

Bernie hears his father's phone click. There is silence. Herman figures his father is satisfied with his string of yeahs.

Friday, Herman goes home as usual for the traditional Friday night meal of chicken soup and roasted chicken with potatoes and carrots. When night settles in Mrs. Milstein says her prayers and lights the sabbath candles. After a quick amen she serves Herman and herself a bowl of soup.

"Where's Dad?" Herman asks.

"He's in New York for a funeral," his mother answers.

"Oh? Who died?" Herman asks.

His mother replies as she spoons some soup to her mouth, "Bernie Katz. Died suddenly."

"Poor Bernie," Herman says.

Merry Memphis Christmas

For Ernie Leibowitz living on the east side of Memphis in 1954 is almost idyllic. There are nearly a dozen boys his age on Stonewall Jackson Circle. He is particularly friends with Butchie Carrington and Billy Wells. Another friend is Willie Turner. His friendship with Willie lasts only a couple months. One day Willie invites him over for a game of Photo Electric Football. Over the mantle is a Nazi flag on either side of which is a Nazi helmet and bayonet.

Ernie asks Willie, "Did your dad get those in the war?"

"No, he belongs to some secret group that waves the flag and uses that other stuff."

When Ernie tells his parents they forbid him to play with Willie any more and restrict him to Stonewall Jackson Circle. So Ernie and Butchie and Billy and some of the other boys play four-on-four football across two front lawns.

When it is Christmas season, one of the boys asks Ernie, "How come y'all don't have Christmas lights or anything?"

"We're Jewish," Ernie responds, "we celebrate *Hanukkah*."

Two nights later a pickup truck with half a dozen men in white sheets and hoods pull up to the Leibowitz home, pour gas in the shape of a cross on the front lawn and set it on fire. It leaves a burned cross on the grass in front of the Leibowitz home.

On the way to school in the morning Billy Wells tells Ernie, "Our parents say it's best y'all leave."

An older boy Ernie does not know says, "Yeah, you best be leavin' the area."

After school Ernie tells his parents who in turn tell Ernie to tell the boys they will be moving after the school year.

Ernie relays the message and the next day during one of their football games Billy tells Ernie, "My daddy says he talked it over with his group of friends and they say the end of the school year will be acceptable."

Roth Learns A Lesson

The day of his mother's funeral Roth dresses in his best suit, neatly ironed white shirt and black tie. His shoes are polished and his hair slicked back. That he is nervous is without doubt. He arrives at the gravesite in his new Oldsmobile Cutlass Calais Quad 4 FE 3 and sees where the casket will be lowered. He gets out and locks the door with the motor running.

The funeral director approaches him and tells him the motor is running in his car. That is when Roth realizes he has locked his keys in the car. The funeral director tells Roth not to worry he has a gravedigger who is just released from prison after three years. "He was a car thief," the director tells Roth.

"And he can open this car?" Roth asks.

"Any car," the funeral director responds.

Roth nods.

The gravedigger is summoned to the car and the problem explained to him. The gravedigger says to Roth, "You want me break in to your car?"

Roth acquiesces and the gravedigger says, "I've never been asked to break in to car. Never thought it was a legal thing to do." The gravedigger studies the car for a moment, asks Roth if the window is manual or electric to which Roth says it is electric.

The gravedigger places his hands on the driver's side power window and lowers it an inch or two, slides one hand in and pulls the window down so he can get both hands on it, then brings it down all the way until he grabs the inside door handle and opens the door. The funeral director and Roth look on with amazement at the gravedigger's talent. The funeral director tells the gravedigger to move the car up a bit so as to accommodate the hearse. The gravedigger puts the car in drive and leaves.

After the burial the funeral director has Roth driven home in the hearse. When he enters his house he finds the place has been ransacked and his valuables and cash gone.

The car is in the garage.

Dig

So, there I was on an archeological dig in Beit She'an, Israel. Previous excavations had been done by the University of Pennsylvania in the 1930s, but here I was almost ninety years later on an Israeli dig to which I had applied and been accepted. My degree is in Semitic Studies from Harvard University and I am employed by the Harvard Semitic Museum. While there was no certainty I would be accepted, my superiors heartily recommended me saying it would be a pleasure being rid of me for three months. I could not tell if they were serious.

Anyway, the flight from Boston to Tel Aviv on El Al was uneventful. We landed around 11 a.m. and I was greeted by a woman holding a sign with my name on it. We quickly exchanged greetings, and she led me to a car, which to my surprise was a Chevy SUV.

It was a two-hour ride to Beit She'an, and my host, Amanda Adar, whose nickname was Manny, pointed to the Tel Aviv skyline—a few *kibbutzim* (collective farms) and some scattered Arab villages. Then the outskirts of Haifa, the main port city which I could see out the car window on the right and if I looked to the left I could see the ocean. We drove past Acco the city with a Crusader castle and fortress nearly one thousand years old. A bit further along was the archaeological site of Megiddo, the biblical Armageddon.

When missionaries first came to what they called the Holy Land, they came to Har Megiddo or the mountain of Megiddo. Since they could not pronounce Har Megiddo, they called it Armageddon.

Then more flat farm land, more Arab villages with their minarets piercing the sky, and a prison built amidst the farms. Finally, we arrived at Beit She'an and went to what Manny said was the best hotel in the city, a three-star facility that would be one star, if that back home.

At the hotel, Manny introduced me to Hanoch Newman and the three of us had dinner, which was typically Israeli: fish, salad, and tea. We retired for the night and Manny told me to be up and ready to go at 5 a.m. as it was really hot by 10. I noticed Manny and Hanoch went to the same room and wondered if they were married or lovers. Either way I thought, *lucky guy*. The next morning, we had a short drive to the *Tel*, a mound which rose above a still-being-excavated Roman city.

"You will know this area goes back to the Neolithic times and was occupied by the Assyrians, Babylonians, Greeks, Romans, Crusaders and Byzantines," Hanoch observed. "You'll be in the tunnel between the amphitheatre and bath houses and you'll probably have it to yourself today. Working in there is good. There is lighting and you won't feel the heat. Temperatures get well over 40 degrees centigrade, and that's more than 100 degrees Fahrenheit."

My first three days in the tunnel were not exciting as the dig there had gone on for months.. The rubble had been cleared out and a few artifacts had been found, I was told. So I was not finding anything archeologically exciting.

The fourth day was the stunner. I had decided to work late and did not realize how long I had been in the tunnel until I emerged. It was so black outside I could barely see a foot or two in front of me and I could not read the time on my wrist watch. The batteries in my cell phone were drained. I looked up to a moonless sky. The Milky Way was stretched across the heavens like a surreal movie. The little light from the stars allowed me to walk toward what had been a grand boulevard in Roman times. It was lined by marble columns when suddenly I bumped into one of the guards.

"Sorry," I said in Hebrew. Getting no response, I tried Arabic. Then Latin, both of which I had studied during college.

Something seemed to have struck a chord and a deep male voice responded in Latin, "No, excuse me."

"Who are you?" I asked.

"Marcellus, guardian of Beit She'an and its treasure," he answered.

Ridiculous, I thought, but who was I to argue with this self-proclaimed Roman guard and his sword? I was scared to death he might use that metal on me. Inside I was shaking like tree branches. Had I eaten bad food or was the night time heat getting to me? Maybe I was just losing my mind. I managed to calm myself. Then in my best collegiate Latin I asked, "Treasure? What treasure?"

"You speak with a strange tongue," the guardian offered, as I saw his hand rest on the sword hilt.

Again, I was scared enough to nearly faint. I quickly offered, "I am from the north of our empire."

"Ah, that might be the reason. But what are you doing here?"

"I was visiting the brothel and fell asleep," I lied, hoping he'd overlook my accent.

He gave a hearty laugh. "Fine women there. I am not allowed to enter though they send the lesser ones to our quarters,"

"And you guard the treasure?" I asked cautiously.

"Yes. Gold, silver, jewels and more in the tunnel. It's behind a stone that was removed and the treasure inserted."

Since the tunnel lights were off, I had the guard lead me to the dig's entrance, where I climbed the fence to exit the grounds. It was not too late so I flagged a passing cab and went to the hotel, grabbed a quick bite, went to my room. I lay in bed staring at the ceiling imagining it was the tunnel. I fell asleep fully clothed.

The sun came up at 3:30 in the morning and I awoke, showered, and dressed. I went downstairs to the lobby waiting for the café to open so I could sip a Turkish coffee along with a bagel or croissant. I took a cab back to the dig, not waiting for Manny or Hanoch. When I got there I hastily walked down the boulevard but did not see the guard. I reported in and hurriedly made my way to the tunnel where the light, which had been strung up along the walls, was lit and I used my flash light to try and find where a stone had been removed and replaced. It took several hours but there was the stone the Roman guard had told me about. It was dark with rough edges. It was easy to cut oneself on the tunnel stones, but not this one. I studied it a few minutes and tried to move it but could not. Then I put the flash light on the floor in front of it and quickly made my way back to the entrance where I found Gabi Hausner, the lead archaeologist, to tell him of my finding. I could not tell him about the Roman guard because he'd think me daft, so I said I happened across it by accident.

Hausner figured there was nothing to lose but time, so he got a half dozen men with heavy metal wedges and we all walked to where I'd left the flashlight. Hausner then set the men to removing the stone.

It took the six men all the strength they could muster to dislodge the embedded rock. When they did, it crashed to the ground leaving a gaping hole that revealed a fortune in gold, silver, jewels and ancient coins. Then shivers ran like mice on my spine because in front of the treasure was a skeleton and on its head sat a helmet like the one the Roman guard, who had revealed the hiding place, had worn.

I Suppose

Being Jewish is not all that bad. I mean, Germany is way behind us and here antisemitism is popular; but not prevailing over those who really do not care one way or the other. There are those who go along, but have no idea why, so as I walk the West End some youngsters throw tomatoes at me. We all laugh as I pullout my .38 Police Special.

Memphis, 1954

Ernie Leibowitz is thirteen when he moves to Memphis because his father gets a job as a cotton plant manager. It is 1954 and the mayor, E.H. Crump, has just died. Segregation rules. Bathrooms, water fountains, seats at the ball park are divided by black and white.

Ernie goes to the ball park on a sunny day before school starts and sees all the good seats are for white people and the edges, left and right field bleachers, are for blacks, if any come. Coming home from the ball park Ernie takes the municipal bus. Having just moved from New York city he does what he always does, he walks straight to the back of the vehicle and sits on the rear bench. He notices everyone on the bus stares at him. The driver pulls over to the curb and walks to the back where Ernie is sitting.

"Can't sit here young man," the driver says.

"Why not? It's empty."

"Only the colored sit here, can't you see? Them coloreds sit in the rear. White folk up front."

Ernie looks at the driver, "That's silly. Where I come from everyone sits where they want."

"Well you ain't where y'all from. You're in Memphis and in Memphis white folk sit up front and the coloreds in the rear. Get it?"

"No," Ernie replies, "I don't, ah, get it."

"You just mosey back up front. There's plenty seats up there and you won't have any trouble."

"Trouble, what kind of trouble?"

"You'll see, I'll call the police."

"I don't believe you, I wanna sit here."

"You can't."

With that the bus driver walks back to the front, removes the keys from the ignition and exits the vehicle, flagging a passing police car. He explains what is happening and one of the policemen comes on the bus. After a quick exchange Ernie finds himself in handcuffs and in the back seat of the black and white cruiser heading to police headquarters.

When his father arrives, the desk sergeant explains what is happening and Ernie's father promises it will not happen again.

Everyday after that Ernie's father drives Ernie to school and a cab waits to take him home.

There Are No Jews In Bloomington

When he moves to Bloomington, Indiana in May, 1955, Chaim Cohen, to his surprise, finds only one synagogue in the town. It houses all the Jewish denominations: Orthodox, Conservative and Reform. He goes to the synagogue where he finds an aging Black janitor.

"Ain't no Jews here anymore," the janitor says. "Last one was driven out of town over a year ago."

"What do I do if I need a synagogue?"

"Gotta go t' Indianapolis, that's where the Jews are. They got them synagogues and temples there."

The next day Cohen moves to Indianapolis.

Encounter

The preacher sits next to me on the plane to Dallas and sees me reading *Archeology of the Bible* and asks me if I am a Christian man. I ignore him and continue reading, but preachers rarely give up, they either want to talk Bible talk or convert you to whatever they preach.

He asks if I am Christian or Catholic and if Christian, which denomination. I smile and say I am Jewish and his face changes. I do not like what I see behind the new look, so I go back to the magazine, but as I said, preachers rarely give up and I could tell this will not be bible talk, but convert talk and I brace for the onslaught hoping I will not get caught with him talking the four hours from New York to Dallas.

He begins slowly, talking about Jesus and how Jesus too had been Jewish until he saw God's light and became a Christian.

So I ask if Jesus is not God himself or maybe at least the son of God, but the preacher says that is Catholic babble and Jesus was a Jew pure and simple; a Jew who sees God's light through a preacher like him named John the Baptist who makes Jesus a Christian.

And, of course, he says that being a Jew I should consider following the King of the Jews footsteps and become what Jesus became.

So I ask if he believes in Jesus having been born of virgin birth as the son of God Almighty and he says that is Catholic babble too yet there is some truth to it and I ask him if that is true how come Jesus was born a Jew and he said God has his way of working things out and the important thing is not what he is born as, but that he died a Christian.

And I ask if Jesus is God, or son of God, or born of virgin birth how can he have brothers and the preacher says it is figure of speech, that all men are brothers to Jesus and that is what makes him so great.

I then ask if he believes Joseph is Mary's uncle and he says of course because the bible says so. So I ask if an uncle humping his niece and creating a baby is incest and the preacher turns red and spittle comes from the corners of his mouth and he coughs and finally says I will never be a Christian.

Maybe not, but the rest of the flight is quiet because the preacher man is lost in his Bible praying for my sin and my soul, because he considers himself a good Christian.

Underpants

There is the day Basil goes to visit Arnie at his home in Brookline. Arnie takes Basil on a nostalgic tour of the old street where both lived some sixty years earlier. Everything is exactly as Basil remembers it: the red brick two story house in which he had lived still has the white columns on the front portico, only the hedges on the front lawn are gone.

It brings Basil thinking back to the 1950s when Brookline kids in his neighborhood give their fathers nicknames. Arnie's father, who lives next door, is called *Undershirt* because on hot days he always sits on the front porch in one of those white tank tops. Then there is Mr. Handleman also lives next door. He is called *Moustache* because he sports one.

There is Basil's father who is the only father without a nickname, that is, until the day his son does something that makes him chase Basil down the front stairs and out into the street while wearing his striped underpants. It seems everyone is outside that late afternoon and all the neighbors laugh. His friends immediately tease Basil about the new nickname *Underpants* which, of course, Basil hates. However, even Basil's family takes to teasing his father, reminding him of that infamous escapade.

Old World Uncles

One smokes, one puts a sugar cube between his teeth when he drinks tea, the third does neither but eats chicken livers sautéed with onion, garlic and rice every night.

Uncle Myron, the smoker, changes cigarette brands every year and dies of lung cancer at age fifty-eight.

Uncle Melvin, the one who loves sugar cubes to sweeten his tea and his coffee, has diabetes which causes his death at age sixty-three.

The one who eats chicken livers, Uncle Levi, dies at sixty-six of a heart attack.

All three had wives who never remarry and live into their nineties.

Chance Meeting

Many years ago I live in Israel for a year and do my best to get into Hebrew University in Jerusalem. As it turns out the tests I take reveal I only have a sixth grade level of Hebrew, so I am unceremoniously denied admission.

Dejected, I wander through the city until exhausted I sit on a park bench. Soon a man wearing a suit and tie, top hat and carrying a walking stick comes along. He sits near me on the bench. Neither of us speak for a few minutes. Then he says hello, and asks why I look so forlorn.

Having only a rudimentary knowledge of Hebrew I do not understand and tell him so. After some questions we discover we can communicate in a combination of Hebrew, English, Yiddish and German. Between the four languages he understanda my predicament and suggests I return to America and go to college. "After a good American college education you will be more useful in Israel.," he says.

It is an issue I am contemplating, to return home or not. After a few minutes I tell him I will take his advice and go home to college.

As I get up to leave he asks my name and when I tell him he asks if I am related to a certain person in the government of Israel. I tell him yes. He tells me to give the man his regards. I say I will and ask his name. "Martin Buber," he says.

Chili Man

Chili Man remembers. He remembers that lunch in the high school cafeteria. He remembers the long table, students seated side by side, like a prison. He remembers that often students sit next to a friend.

Some students bring their own lunch, often peanut butter and jelly, but that day Mark Sheinblum, aka, Chili Man, buys a bowl of chili along with desert and soda. He walks with it all on a tray and as he goes behind me with the tray over my head someone says something that makes me jump up, my head hitting the bottom of the tray that Chili Man carries. It makes the bowl of chili on his tray flip over and land on him. He stands there with the chili oozing down over his shirt which, of course, makes every student, even the monitors and some of the teachers in the cafeteria laugh and point at him. Chili Man begins scooping it off his shirt. His friend Melvin Schwartz laughs and points at him so Chili Man takes it off his shirt and patting it on Melvin who responds by doing it back to Chili Man. Pretty soon they have their own private food fight until Chili Man remembers who causes the chili to land on him. He stops and stares at me, his face now dripping with chili. I see him glower and the thoughts in his head as he turns toward me. My feet are already moving when I see the look on his face: eyes narrow, arms reaching out for me. I push over a chair between us so he has to hurdle it or go around, giving me the seconds I need for a head start. He gets even angrier because most of the students in the cafeteria are laughing even harder.

Oh, how I run. Chili Man never has a chance to catch me.

Now fifty years later at the high school reunion he says, "I would have killed you if I had caught you."

But it is fifty years later and we laugh about what had seemed like a life changing event. Now, just a joke between Chili Man and me.

I do believe that had he reached me, I would not be here today to tell this story.

... and Guns

Stand at the iron gate where work makes one free, where free means death. Death is for them to leave the world naked as they came into the world.

It is a world they know is no longer theirs. They stand before the gaping pits of hell where men in gray with guns direct them to the edge of forever. There are gray clouds and the sound of guns.

Best Foot Forward

Herschel Greppsel is a rather sickly child, his pale skin often pink with fever. His eyes, the deep brown of his Russian parentage, are constantly tinged by the red watery symptoms of the frequent colds that encumber his nose with difficult breathing and sniffles.

At the first sign of abnormal inhalation his mother rushes to Golmeyer the butcher to purchase a good cooking chicken and boils the fowl for soup. By age ten Herschel grows to despise chicken soup, more for its medicinal associations than his immense consumption of it.

In fact, in their tenement in the Roxbury section of Boston where five other families share a three-story brick building on Hutchings Street, the youngsters his age utter "mamma" or "papa" as their first words. Young Greppsel says, "Chicken soup." It is not a statement or a question, but more of a burp.

"What?" Goldie Greppsel is not hard of hearing. Yankel her husband maintains that her excessive weight coupled with her large bosoms has an effect on her hearing.

"Chicken soup," the nineteen-month-old infant repeats, and follows the historic occasion with a quick sniffle that causes Goldie to reply *Gesundtheit*, lift him off the floor, tuck her son under her right arm and rush to Sadie Minchink across the hall to deposit him there while she dashes off to Golmeyer's for a good cooking chicken.

It was not until she skims the fat off the top of the soup, carefully tests the bird with a fork and dumps in a load of egg noodles in the pot that Goldie realizes her son speaks.

Herschel is already nestled beneath two blankets and a quilt, thermometer in his mouth so is unable to utter another word.

Goldie Greppsel quickly wipes her hands on the apron she wears avoiding its frilly edges, but smearing the front where her bosom protrudes with partially cooked chicken soup, a shred of carrot, a slice of celery and some onion skin. Her bosom, in fact, is so large that none of these items fall from her as she walks toward her son's room pride swelling her breasts even more, so that anyone seeing her now is certain they will explode and leave smatterings all over the five room apartment.

When he is 10 in 1952, Herschel Greppsel catches a virus. His colds stop coming and he leads a perfectly normal life, walking by himself three houses up the street to the Garrison School. He buys baseball cards at Schlossberg's Apothecary and trades duplicates with other children in the neighborhood.

But then the ear infection. It lasts nine months and Yankel jokes it is like Mrs. Vogel downstairs, whose belly begins to swell about the same time Herschel first notices his ear ache. The illness ends simultaneously with the birth of Seymour Vogel.

For the entire infectious period Dr. Vishniak prescribes earmuffs, which Herschel is forced to wear throughout the nine month ordeal, compounded by Mrs. Greppsel's insistence he wear an overcoat whenever he goes out, even in warm weather. Herschel rebels but Yankel ends the dispute by issuing his edict that the youngster comply and suggests, as compensation, the use of sunglasses to hide his identity.

Herschel is seen on Hutchings Street, Humboldt Avenue and Elm Hill Avenue wearing black earmuffs, a dark blue overcoat and green sunglasses. He adds a beige hat and tells everyone he is an FBI agent assigned to uncover young communists. Yankel tells him he is crazy and so is Joe McCarthy, but Herschel tells his father to leave him alone or he will report him. To Herschel's amazement, Yankel complies.

At 14, Herschel barely clears five feet and his friends bully him unmercifully. He has few female friends and most of the snickering girls are at least two inches taller. All except Mildred Krasnick who at four feet, nine inches is the brunt of more jokes than Herschel. He likes Mildred because she is the one person he can tease.

Unfortunately for them, he finds the flat chested girl a reincarnation of a shtetl woman he saw in a book of old world Jewish painting his parents kept in the living room. The woman in the book has a hooked nose, kinky hair, rounded hips and an overall rating of unappealing.

At the end of Herschel's freshman year in high school Yankel sends his son to Israel for the summer. The trip is promised as a Bar Mitzvah gift and it takes every effort to make the old man keep his promise since Herschel faints five times on Friday night causing Rabbi Asgood ("As good as any rabbi," the cleric likes to tell people) to bring smelling salts on Saturday morning and Goldie to arrive at the synagogue with a small jar of chicken soup in the event her son collapses again.

But Israel is the promise kept. The trip puts the family in debt but allows Herschel to maintain his social status with his friends, most of whom are part of an AZA youth trip to a kibbutz on the shores of the Sea of Galilee. It is a wonderful two months. In July everyone works in the cow shed, shovels chicken manure, works in the garden, irrigates fields and learns Hebrew. They awake at three-thirty in the morning, about one-half hour before sunrise and head to their assignments. They labor until seven, eat breakfast in the communal dining hall and at eight return to work for three hours before walking back to the dining hall for lunch.

It is the summer love bloomed. Harry Shulman necks with Janey Chafetz. Sammy Greenberg boasts he had grabbed a feel of Betty Polsky's breasts and starts a rush that makes Betty the most popular girl of the group. But not all the boys succeed. Sumner Karp is rejected by three girls because they suspect that being a doctor's son he knows too much about the anatomy.

As for Herschel, no one notices until he returns home that he has grown a full foot now an even six feet. He is so skinny he no longer enjoys swimming because his ribs resemble an emaciated Brahmin bull that serves as the background for an even more starvation racked Mahatma Gandhi whose picture adorns his bathroom wall.

The Greppsels now live in Newton along with many of their friends from the old neighborhood. They are transplants from Roxbury where blacks move in to replace the Jews just as the Jews displace the Irish who take over when the old Yankees abandon the area.

His thinness bothers him so much that one afternoon reading a comic book he carefully reviews a Charles Atlas advertisement and pictures himself as the skinny guy who has sand kicked in his face.

"Hey pop," Herschel asks his father, "do you suppose Charles Atlas is Jewish?"

"Everyone is Jewish until proven innocent," the old man responds and Herschel thinks his father is a true philosopher. Yankel is also a dictator who never allows his son to conduct business with anyone who is not Jewish.

"The *goyim* take care of themselves and never come to us so why shouldn't we return the compliment?" Yankel reasons.

Since his father has not indicated that Charles Atlas is a goy, Herschel assumes the muscle man is Jewish and sends his dime for a brochure followed by a dollar ninety-eight for the full Dynamic Tension course. Faithfully each day the skinny disciple with crew cut hair adheres to the teachings of his master. Within months he is muscle bound, free of illness, hair not too long or too short. He is popular with the girls, as Charles Atlas predicted in a personal letter to Herschel when the boy graduates the course. Herschel wonders if the he-man's real name is Atlasavitch.

At 20, Herschel, whose father stresses education over athletics, finds himself a junior at Harvard. He really does not fit in with many of the snobby, pseudo-intellects who dot the campus and share Herschel's fraternity, college residence and classrooms. One night at a fraternity party—he pledges Sigma Epsilon Xi—after he has a few frat grogs, he approaches a beautiful coed. She is short to be sure, but her blonde hair, aquiline nose and full breasts attract him instantly. Herschel and the blonde dance, talk and dance some more. Herschel has a few more grogs and plies the blonde with a few as well.

He finally asks her name and she says, "Diane."

"You look familiar, like I've known you before," Herschel says.

"That's a lousy line but true," she responds.

"I certainly wouldn't forget a beautiful girl like you," Herschel says, trying to sound like a suave fraternity upperclassman. He is happy to dance and speak with her after she rejects all those who try to meet her.

Despite the alcohol he can tell she is pert. "Okay, okay, where'd we meet?"

"We shared a room once," Diane tells him with a smile that Hersh, as he is now known, decides is more teasing than humorous. "In Israel," she adds with a wink and whirls around, heading for the bar with a wiggle that forces Hersh to follow.

"Wait a minute, where the hell do I know you from?"

"Ah, you rejected once, twice, thrice," she answers.

"Never one as beautiful as you. Impossible." He gulps down another grog. It is his fifth or maybe sixth.

"Well if I tell you my name is Mildred Krasnick, will that ring a bell?"

Herschel looks perplexed so the blonde continues, "My name is Mildred Diane Krasnick. My family moved from Roxbury because my father owns an electronics factory and made a fortune. We stayed in Newton only one year and then moved to Weston. Daddy got me a nose job from a big doctor and I began using my middle name since it's a little more modern, you know. I did bust exercises every night to build up my chest and I used Clairol on my hair. I also managed to get into Radcliff."

Hersh tells her she is beautiful. Flattered she confesses she has liked him since the fourth grade back at the Garrison School. They talk as they move toward the staircase up to his room where they make love for the first time. In the morning his sobriety returns and he awakes to find that Mildred Diane Krasnick looks exactly the way she did in the ninth grade.

"What happened to the blond hair?" Hersh wailed. "Your chest exercises? Is your father a millionaire? Are you at Radcliff? Mildred, what happened?" Hersh is beside himself, or to his horror beside Mildred.

"Gee, think you're mixing me up with one of my sorority sisters. Or maybe you imagined something when you were drunk," Mildred tells him. She snuggles up to him and squeals with pleasure from their night together.

"Impossible," Hersh says trying not to insult the woman whose virginity he has extracted to the last ounce. He can barely remember anything, thanks to the old Sigma Epsilon Xi grog, blended in the ancient tradition.

"It is Mildred Krasnick and I have always loved you. I think it's wonderful you turned out to be a handsome prince and we found each other. You have made me very happy," Mildred tells him as she moves toward him for a kiss. Hersh, trying to keep distance between them, rolls off the bed as he attempts to avoid her pursed lips.

Three months later Mildred, not having heard from Hersh, calls to tell him she is very pregnant. Three weeks later Mildred Krasnick becomes Mildred Greppsel.

When he is 25, Herschel is now the father of two girls, Darla and Marla, both of whom by age five display the same unattractive features that are the hallmark of their mother's physical features. He rarely goes out in public with Mildred.

Hersh, Harvard degree hanging on the bedroom wall, receives contributions from Mildred's father and Yankel, uses the money to open a shoe store where he handles curved arches with tender caresses while ignoring the passes from women who find his touch erotic. Hersh can spot a good foot the minute it walks in the door. A particularly well formed pair attracts him so much that he has to find just the right shoe and hold the dainty toes in his hand, coax it gently into a stylish shoe which he especially selects for each woman.

But he is also a man so it is inevitable that when a truly exquisite foot enters his store he spots it immediately. It is a right foot, perfectly formed with straight toes that are rather long, almost like Arthur Rubenstein's fingers. Hersh knows they are meant for the best instrument he has to comfort and enhance them.

As he attempts to fit the foot he gently feels the ankle, the heel and ball and with great sensitivity lowers it into the shoe. Hersh is fortunate. It is nearly closing time so he shuts down three minutes early and follows the feet wherever they go.

It turns out there is no need to follow since the feet give him a magical signal that scream, "Come, come with us!"

As he lays in bed licking the arch, kissing the Achilles tendon and sucking the toes, he knows he has found bliss and will never let these feet leave. They are not fat or bony. They do not have an offensive odor. The skin is smooth. They are the pair of feet in a million.

The affair lasts nearly a year during which Hersh is forced to make hundreds of different excuses for not going home or not being at the store when Mildred or his daughters call or drop in. One evening Mildred confronts Hersh and he confesses it all.

He moves out the next morning, sleeping on a cot at the back of the store.

At age 30, Hersh agonizes over the Vietnam War. He falls under the influence of Kitty Katz, a left winger who publishes an underground newsletter for draft dodgers instructing them how to leave the United States and not be caught. She informs them how they can avoid being hunted down. There are times Hersh feels Kitty is really an FBI informer, but since he agrees with her antiwar sentiments he does not care, especially since she also believes in free love.

His hair now shoulder length, Hersh is summoned before the draft board for a physical which he flunks, ironically, because of flat feet—the worst the Army has ever seen—he is told.

Eventually Hersh leases his shoe store to a Greek who speaks little English but can stroke a calf well and, therefore, keeps the business going. Hersh takes to wearing blue jeans and plaid, flannel shirts no matter the season. He grows a moustache and beard and for a while during early 1974 fancies himself a latter day messiah, often standing in front of the statue of John Harvard on the campus of his alma mater telling students to forsake war and accept religion.

The administration does not have the heart to remove an alumnus from their property, especially one who still contributes handsomely to the annual fund drive. It matters little to them what he looks like and since he is not preaching against the university and as long as his money keeps coming, the administration ignores him.

Hersh finally gives up his outdoor pulpit when the president of Harvard approaches, "Greppsel, are you religious?"

Hersh is taken aback. How can this exalted leader remember him by name? As always Hersh knows he will have to tell the truth. He becomes a truth teller the day his mother nearly smothers him by pressing his face into her huge, sagging bosom and paddling him with the wood stirring spoon which she yanks from the chicken soup pot.

Hersh admits he is not religious. The president of Harvard looks at him benevolently and says, "Leave! Get off my property you hypocrite. Reclaim your shoe business. Make money. Develop a shoe empire. And above all, increase your donation to the annual giving fund."

Hersh nods meekly and walks off puffing on marijuana Kitty Katz says will allow him to see the world more clearly.

At 35, Hersh has his empire: 27 Greppsel Shoe Stores in 18 communities in the greater Boston area. He believes his slogan, *If The Shoe Fits, Wear It* is the key to success, along with the personal service and fine quality leather shoes he sells. Hersh's idea of personal service means that he himself drops in on a different store each day, sometimes two stores, bends his knee and sells shoes just the way he had thirteen years earlier when he opened his first store.

Hersh's hair is now neatly coiffed by a stylist. He has a penchant for three-piece suits, wing tip shoes, and a carnation in each lapel, a silk handkerchief in the breast pocket, striped ties and a Harvard accent. One of his store managers tells a subordinate who is perplexed, that Hersh was so formal he probably sleeps in three-piece pajamas. And of course, Hersh has upped his annual giving to Harvard considerably and serves on their finance committee. He is a paragon of the community. The president of Harvard calls him Mr. Greppsel and asks if he might call him Herschel.

One afternoon Herschel, who still searches for the perfect foot, encounters one. It is a dream come true. The foot is perfectly formed, with smooth white skin, clear, well trimmed toenails that are free from polish and bones that do not protrude. The ankle is round and firm, the heel well rounded, the ball plump, but not fat. He follows the foot up to a lovely calf and peeks under the skirt at a stupendous thigh. It is the best leg he has ever come across.

The pinkish flush which comes to his cheeks ebbs as he lifts his head and his eyes meet those of the woman who belongs to those feet. His natural color returns, but this time with a deeper shade of embarrassment. It is Mildred. She smiles at him and he sits next to her and they talk. She has never remarried and has only gone on a few dates since they divorce. Looking at her, Hersh can understand why no man wants her unless he takes the time to study her feet. He invites her to lunch and takes her hand to lead her toward the door. He notices her hand is as perfect as her foot. As they walk toward the restaurant Hersh begins thinking about opening a glove section in his store.

About the Authors

Paul Beckman's flash collection, *Kiss Kiss,* was a finalist for the 2019 Indie Short Story Award competition. Paul was nominated by *Citron Review* for Best Microfiction 2020 and had a micro story selected for the *2018 Norton Anthology New Micro Exceptionally Short Fiction.* He was one of the winners in the 2016 *The Best Small Fictions* and his story "Mom's Goodbye" was chosen as the winner of the *2016 Fiction Southeast* Editor's Prize.

Zvi A. Sesling, Brookline, MA Poet Laureate (2017-2020), has published numerous poems and flash fiction. He edits *10 By 10 Flash Fiction Stories* and *Muddy River Poetry Review.* He is author of five poetry books and two chapbooks. Sesling was first prize winner in the Reuben Rose International Poetry Competition. He's been nominated for five Pushcart Prizes., and other national and local awards.

Made in the USA
Middletown, DE
12 October 2024

62513784R00064